Jubilee Year

Other books by Margaret Evans Porter

IRISH AUTUMN
ROAD TO RUIN

Jubilee Year

Margaret Evans Porter

Walker and Company
New York

First published in the United States of America in 1991 by
Walker Publishing Company, Inc.
Published simultaneously in Canada by Thomas Allen & Son
Canada, Limited, Markham, Ontario

Library of Congress Cataloging-in-Publication Data
Porter, Margaret Evans
Jubilee Year: a Regency novel / Margaret Evans Porter
p.   cm.
ISBN 0-8027-1167-7
I. Title.
PS3566.O653J8   1991
813'.54—dc20   91-8612
CIP

Printed in the United States of America

2   4   6   8   10   9   7   5   3   1

King George's Fiftieth Year
Of Sceptred greatness cheer
  Each loyal Heart;
May the stain'd Sword be sheathed;
Amity once more breath'd;
Commerce, with Plenty wreath'd,
  Sweet Joy impart.

Jubilee Song for 25 October, 1809
Tune: "God Save the King"

Jubilee Year

= PROLOGUE =

THE SILVER COLUMNS of the birches reached skyward, as if to touch the ominous, low-hanging clouds. Justin Blythe was thankful for the leather boots which encased his legs almost to the knee, permitting him to proceed through the deepest drifts with no ill effect. His thick greatcoat, fashioned in the cossack style and lined with sable, protected him from the bitter wind, and he wore a hat of black bearskin. Only his lean, fine-boned face was exposed to the elements as he trudged on, heedless of flakes falling around him. The virgin snow gave way beneath his feet, retaining the deep impression of each step. When he paused to catch his breath, he heard the persistent ring of an axe on wood.

Born and bred in England, he'd never really grown accustomed to Russia's colder and fiercer climate. Faced with the prospect of leaving his adopted land before very much longer, he could at least look forward to arriving in his own country in time to see the full flowering of its glorious spring.

He turned to survey the visible sign of his progress, his farsighted eyes tracing the long chain of footprints stretching from the wood all the way across the park to the domed winter palace. Someone was following him— he could see a distant figure, small and dark and insignificant against the blanket of snow. Justin curtailed his expedition and went to meet his pursuer.

As soon as he was within earshot he called out, in his best schoolmaster fashion, "Have you abandoned your lessons, Feodor Pavlovich?"

1

"*Maman* gave me permission to come." The dark-haired boy reached beneath his long cloak and withdrew a square of folded paper. "This has just arrived for you," he announced. "From England!"

Justin held the long-travelled missive at arm's length, squinting as he tried to decipher the blurred handwriting. It belonged to his mother.

When he tucked the letter into the pocket of his greatcoat, Prince Feodor Levaskov asked in surprise, "Aren't you going to read it?"

"I haven't my spectacles with me."

They fell into step together, man and child; both were silent, their faces thoughtful.

"Why must you leave us, *monsieur*?" the boy asked as they proceeded back to the Levaskov palace. "I thought you were happy at Droskoe." His English was carefully precise and only faintly accented.

"I have been very happy here," Justin replied, "but it is time I returned to my own home."

After a moment Feodor looked up again. "And when you have left, which of us will you miss more, me or Ivanushka?"

"Well," said Justin consideringly, "you are greatly improved from when I first came to live with your papa and mama, but your little brother is undoubtedly an engaging fellow, and I've known him since the day he was born. I'll have to write from England and let you know the answer."

Looking up, the boy caught the the gleam of mischief in his preceptor's brown eyes. "Ah, but you jest, *monsieur*," he said in relief. "But," he added, "I have another question, and this time you must give a serious answer."

"I shall strive to do so."

"Do you think I am clever enough for an English school?"

"Is it your ambition to attend one?" When Justin's companion responded with a vigorous and determined nod, he said, "If you went away to school, you'd have to leave your mother and Ivanushka."

"Yes, but if *Maman* wishes it . . ." After a pause, the child said with affected carelessness, "I would not be so very lonely. And you could sometimes visit me."

"That is true," Justin agreed.

"After you go, I mean to follow very closely my schedule of studies. If *Maman* decides that I must go to school in England, I do not want to displease her by not being prepared."

Fingering the letter in his pocket, Justin reflected that his young friend had already learned how a man's destiny could be ruled by his duty to his mother.

As the honoured guest of Princess Natalia Levaskov, Justin lived as if he were a prince. Upon first taking up residence at Droskoe, the crimson hangings, ornate rococo furniture, and velvet upholstery had seemed overpowering; now he was so accustomed that he seldom noticed the lavishness of his surroundings. Upon his return from his walk, he sought the privacy of a handsome parlour and sat down at an elegant writing desk. He picked up a pair of gold-rimmed spectacles and put them on to read his mother's letter. It was directed to Viscount Cavender, the title he had held for less than a year. The Bath postmark was fully three months old. Breaking the seal, he unfolded the single sheet and scanned the neat, even lines. Just as he'd expected, his parent entreated him to return to England, and the context made it clear that his last attempt to communicate with her had gone astray. Given the present state of war between England and Russia, it was not surprising.

Starved for word from his family and friends, he savoured each morsel of news, even though he knew them to be stale, and only after he'd read the letter through twice did he remove his eyeglasses. He glanced towards the nearest window, which was double-glazed to prevent drafts. Through the coating of frost on the outer pane he could make out the woodcutter and a horse-drawn sledge piled high with fuel for the stoves which kept the Levaskov palace so comfortably warm.

Three years ago, Justin, a younger son with no money and few prospects for advancement in his own country, had come to Russia as a secretary to British Ambassador Lord Granville Leveson-Gower and had remained there after his superior was recalled. His lordship's replacement was less amiable and unpopular with English and Russians alike, so the British government prevailed upon Lord Granville to undertake a special and sensitive mission. The negotiations, in which Justin had taken a small part, had not prospered. Emperor Alexander, after his conference with Napoleon Bonaparte on the raft at Tilsit, elected to make his treaty with France rather than England. Russia had severed diplomatic relations with her old ally, who retaliated by declaring war.

The British delegation speedily decamped, and still Justin had stayed behind. He joined the vast household of his friend Prince Paul Levaskov, moving with the family from townhouse to summer palace to winter palace as the seasons dictated. He hunted wolves and played cards and courted the handsomest actresses in Moscow, and he took on the not very arduous task of tutoring his host's young son. But he'd also found another kind of employment: his observations of Russian society and any news of military manoeuvres which came to him found their way into the reports he complied for the Foreign Office. A Dutch banker, a resident of Moscow with connexions in London, arranged to have them smuggled through Amsterdam.

Last summer, when Justin had learned of his only brother's sudden and unexpected death, he had intended to depart for England at once, but his plans were postponed when Prince Paul succumbed to a debilitating fever which eventually took his life. Justin's loyalty to the widowed princess, heavy with child, and his fondness for the grieving Feodor imposed an indefinite delay on his departure from Russia.

He looked away from the window. A young woman had entered the parlour, and at the sight of her black-clad figure, the straight, taut line of his mouth curved into a smile. Stepping from behind the ormolu table, he said jovially, "So, Natasha, am I to place your princeling in one of my trunks and convey him to England for you?"

"That would be an adventure Feo would much enjoy." Princess Natalia Levaskov's accent was rather more pronounced than her son's, but to Justin's ears it was charming. She had softly curling hair, bright hazel eyes, and her small, well-rounded body still bore faint traces of her recent confinement. "Yet you need not take the trouble," she went on, "for I may go to England myself, after the summer. I must settle affairs here and on my other estates, but when that is done I think you will see all of us again—Feo and Ivanushka and me."

"This is welcome news," Justin told her, smiling, "but it seems a sudden decision."

"Less sudden than you think. My cousin lives there—Catherine Woronzov, who married the Lord Pembroke. And Prince Paul had an English grandmother. He intended we should make a visit to our relatives when Feo would be old enough for the journey, but then the war broke out." Natasha cast a sweeping and comprehensive glance around the room and said in a tone of disparagement, "We Russians fill our houses with French furniture and paintings, and we ape Parisian fashions. We even prefer to speak French at Court and in our salons. But France is still the enemy, despite our emperor's treaty with Bonaparte. England is surely safer, for who can say how long that Corsican beast will prey upon Europe? He is greedy; he may well try to subdue Russia in time. I would send Feo to a military school, but as we are now an ally of France he might someday be required to fight on behalf of the man so much despised by his father. That I could not permit," she said firmly.

"No, of course not."

She sat down upon a tufted bench ornamented with gold tassels and announced, "Feo is to be educated at Harrow."

"Not Eton?" asked an aggrieved Justin. "Natasha, you wound me."

"Harrow is where Prince Paul's cousins were," she said

apologetically. "But Ivanushka will go to school where you wish, I promise."

"So it is not farewell for us, after all," he said, regarding her fondly, "but merely *au revoir*."

"You are glad?" His ready nod brought a blush to Natasha's plump cheek. "The months we are apart will pass slowly for me," she sighed, "and I fear I will find you changed when we meet again. Will not your mother turn you into a proper English, milord?"

"You may depend upon her trying," he answered. "But I lack most of the necessary accoutrements, for my brother left me little more than his title. My estate in Wiltshire is leased by a retired merchant and has been for nearly twenty years."

Tipping her head to one side, she said, "Perhaps Lady Cavender has already found for you a rich wife."

Justin shook his head and sent a stray lock of brown hair tumbling onto his brow. "England is not so very different from Russia. The only girls likely to cast out lures to an impoverished viscount will be the ones who are hopelessly plain, or those whose papas are in trade. The former would not appeal to me, and the latter will never be acceptable to my mother. I vow you'll find me still a bachelor when you set foot on English soil."

As Natasha gazed back at him so silently and steadily, Justin could not be sure whether he read relief or skepticism in her expression.

She had been one of society's butterflies when he had met her, an accomplished flirt who was much admired by the gentlemen of the emperor's court. From the onset of her husband's illness she had lived in seclusion at Droskoe, but Justin had been conscious of her increasing restlessness of late, perhaps because it paralleled his own. His long residence in her household, coupled with the recent birth of her son Ivan, had led to a disturbing rumour which was still, he suspected, making the rounds of the fashionable salons in St. Petersburg and Moscow. If he did not leave her, he would be obliged to wed her.

"When do you go?" she asked, breaking the silence.

"As soon as possible, perhaps within the week. But until I reach St. Petersburg, I won't know my prospects for swift transport to England." Because his tie to her was one of affection as well as convenience and mutual dependence, he regretted the necessity of separation. But it would not be a long one, and from that they could both take comfort.

=1=

FROM THE MOMENT Lady Miranda Peverel stepped across the threshold of Solway House, her guardian's London residence, she found herself at the centre of a storm of activity. She entered into the preparations for her birthday ball with what passed for eagerness but was actually an attempt to hide her lingering doubts about coming to town. In the days preceding the great event, she was seized by a craven desire to celebrate her natal day as she had always done, in the comfortable and familiar seclusion of Haberdine Castle in Northamptonshire.

From a disinclination to add to the monstrous expense her uncle had already incurred, and her dislike of being at the beck and call of some fashionable dressmaker, Miranda had dispensed with the purchase of a new gown. Her aunt, with so many details to oversee, raised no very strenuous objection to this plan.

"It makes no odds what you wear, for you look well in almost anything," the duchess commented on the eve of what would be the first grand ball of the Season. She sat as motionless as a statue as her woman deftly arranged her fine black hair, which had recently begun to show some threads of silver. "But you must settle on a gown at once if Bleaklow is to make whatever alterations may be required."

Miranda curtsied and replied, "If you will excuse me, Aunt, I'll see to it at once."

She went down the long hall to a spacious bedchamber, where she found her own abigail rearranging a selection of spring bonnets on the topmost shelf of a wardrobe. "Never mind that, Agnes," Miranda said, her blue eyes bright, "we have a more important task at hand."

Within the hour the duchess visited her niece's room to inspect her choice of gown. Miranda stood upon a low stool, her slim figure draped in pearl-colored silk, while the abigail knelt on the floor like a supplicant before a young queen, pinning a flounce to the hem. With an approving nod, the duchess commented, "The notion of silver lace edging is a good one."

Miranda lowered her dark head to smile down at her middle-aged handmaiden. "The credit for that goes to Agnes."

"I daresay. Well," said her aunt, "you ought to have had a new gown, but not a soul in London will recognise it, or guess that it's last year's. It's too simple to be out of mode."

For nearly a decade she had stood in place of a mother to Miranda, and her grey eyes shone with maternal pride as they rested upon the delicate oval face with its rosy lips and faintly cleft chin. Today Agnes had threaded an indigo ribbon through the silky black locks, as though Miranda were still a girl, although she would attain her majority tomorrow. Her youthful spirits had been subdued by time, for the setbacks and disappointments of recent years had left their mark, but the duchess, seeing her niece arrayed in bridal white and silver, was hopeful of a happier future. With a satisfied smile, she sailed out of the room to see to other pressing matters.

Agnes Bleaklow resumed her work. Miranda jumped at the insistent thudding of the door-knocker. Around the pins in her mouth, Agnes said, "If you hop about so, your lace will be crooked, my lady, and then what a figure you'll look!"

Miranda resumed her stiff pose, but dropped it altogether when a footman in livery came to inform her that the Marquis of Elston awaited her in the conservatory.

"But, my lady," Agnes cried when Miranda stepped

down from her pedestal, "you can't receive his lordship with pins sticking out of you, and in the very gown you'll be wearing tomorrow night!"

"Of course I can," Miranda contradicted her blithely. "Besides, he's seen it already, at Christmas."

"Your ladyship ought to be ashamed to admit it," the abigail grumbled.

At the bottom of the great marble staircase, Miranda paused before a Venetian mirror to pass one hand over her hair, slightly disarranged by the taking off and putting on of a succession of gowns. She proceeded to the back of the house and opened the glass-paned door of the conservatory.

Lord Elston seemed to have been created for the purpose of serving as Miranda's complement, for he was as tall and fair as she was small and dark. His aristocratic head was crowned with shining blonde hair, and the handsome face was marred only by the chill in the depths of his eyes, nearly as blue as Miranda's own. They thawed perceptibly at her entrance, and when she extended her hand he seized it and pulled her close to kiss her cheek.

"Damon, really!" she protested, wriggling until he released her.

"Don't you like that style of greeting?"

"I'm not sure that I do," she answered tartly, "and I can't think why my aunt and uncle permit me to receive you unchaperoned. You are a shocking creature!"

"But such an old friend that you'll forgive my presumption."

"Only because I'm so very glad to see you again—it has been an age since Christmas. Knowing your dislike of the country, I recognised your visit to Haberdine as the great sacrifice it was." And when he replied that it had been no such thing, she shook her head. "You always make light of your kindnesses. My gratitude knows no bounds, and—and I *wish* I knew how to thank you," she concluded, her voice shaking with emotion. Her cleft chin trembled slightly as her blue eyes misted over with tears.

"Be easy, Mira," Damon said in a soothing tone. He was well enough acquainted with her to be aware of her extreme sensibility, and he also knew what a trial it was to her. In the hope of diverting her, he complimented her gown, saying, "Very pretty, to be sure, though it seems to be falling apart at the edges. A new fashion, I devoutly hope?"

Miranda, following the direction of his gaze, discovered that the lace on her puffed sleeves was slipping from its pins and gave a weak laugh. After assuring him that she would present a more creditable appearance tomorrow, she sat down upon a curved bench at the base of a potted palm tree, and with a careless wave of her hand indicated that he should do the same. "You're always such a fountain of town news, and I've not yet heard the latest. Do tell me everything."

"Hell is empty, and all the devils are here," Damon drawled. "London is consumed with gossip at the moment—I wrote to tell you about the Mary Anne Clarke affair, I believe. No doubt you followed the progress of the Duke of York's trial in the papers. But you may not know that Lord Falkland fought a duel with Pogey Powell and was killed—they quarrelled while drunk. Lord Paget has abandoned his wife to elope with Henry Wellesley's. There is to be a grand jubilee in October, to mark the fiftieth year of His Majesty's reign." He furrowed his marble-white brow, then produced another tidbit. "The Whip Club has just voted to rechristen itself the Four-in-Hand Club, so we're having new buttons cast. The toggery has been altered as well, and the driving coat is to be white drab with fifteen capes, but I daresay this news will interest your cousin Gervase far more than it does you. Will he be in town? Our first meeting is set for the end of the month."

"He's fixed at Shropshire just now," Miranda reported, "which is a pity. What fun the three of us had at Christmas, with our impromptu concerts!"

"I've restrung my violin in the expectation that our recital would be repeated. Perhaps the duchess can be persuaded to give a musical party, that we may show off our talents."

"I don't doubt that she would if I asked her," Miranda said. "But I fear I spent more time on horseback this winter than I did practising the pianoforte! Besides, you'll be too busy with your own amusements."

"I won't neglect you, *chérie*, now that you've deigned to grace the metropolis with your so-charming self. I couldn't bear it if you bolted back to the wilds of Northamptonshire."

"I won't do that, you may be sure. Unless," she amended with a quelling glance, "you persist with these foolish gallantries. Don't think you can pawn your town tricks off on me—*I'm* not one of your flirts."

There was a laugh in his eye, but he said meekly, "Yes, my lady. Or rather, no. Tell me, for you failed to do so in your last letter, just why do you come to London? I'd quite given up hope of seeing you on my own turf, much less during the Season."

"I'm here to find myself a husband, if there are any to be had."

This matter-of-fact explanation surprised Damon, who had believed her to be as set against wedlock as he was himself. "Well, well," he murmured, narrowing his eyes. "You never struck me as being marriage-mad."

"Till now I wasn't. And I wasn't at all sure I could bear the revival of old scandals. But in the end I decided that I had to come if I truly wanted to lay them to rest. Which I do," she said fervently. "It's not that I'm unhappy with my aunt and uncle, but they have sheltered me so long, and now I'm twenty-one. As a married woman, I would have an establishment of my very own, I would be assured of companionship and employment. My father is dead, my brother is but a schoolboy, and my mother . . ." After a brief pause she concluded, "And my mother is popularly believed to be a madwoman."

Damon saw no signs of the tears that so often betrayed her, although her lovely face was pensive when she said, "Before that unfortunately public scene in Bath, people were so careful to employ polite euphemisms when speaking of her affliction. I don't doubt there are those who suspect she passed it down to me—another reason I felt it was necessary to end my days as a recluse. And though she seldom mentions it, I'm sure Aunt Elizabeth worries that if I don't marry soon, I may never. So, my dear friend, I've come to town. Now, please let's talk of other matters."

"Here's a bit of news I forgot," Damon said brightly. "My cousin Justin has returned. I've had word that his ship docked at Yarmouth two days ago, and I expect to see him in Berkeley Square shortly."

"I don't remember meeting him," Miranda mused, "although his brother often spoke of him. Why don't you bring Lord Cavender to our party, if he arrives in time?"

"Thank you, I will." Damon picked up his gloves and climbed to his feet. "I only meant to look in for a moment, for I suspect you have no time to waste on me today. My respects to the duke, and to your aunt—I look forward to seeing them tomorrow evening. And you had better save a dance or two for me, or you'll regret it!"

"Of course I shall, for I depend upon you to keep me from being a wallflower at my own ball!"

When she gave him her hand at parting, he raised it to his lips, then said in a caressing voice, "That is hardly likely to occur. I predict that you'll have your husband by the Season's end, if finding one is truly your heart's desire."

Damon left Solway House to find the clouds dissipated; the breeze was flavoured by the April freshness of Hyde Park, overpowering the pervasive stench of the Thames. He enjoyed walking the streets of his beloved London, so he ignored the several hackney coaches waiting at the corner of Park Lane and Mount Street and strolled in the direction of Berkeley Square. As usual, his tall, elegant figure drew stares, for he was a well-known personage. He was often described as one of the most handsome men of his generation; certainly he was one of the wealthiest. A fixture in London, and a popular one, he received invitations to every fashionable ball, dinner, and rout, and his illustrious name could be found on rosters of a number of exclusive clubs and societies. Yet he possessed only a few close friends, and during his twenty-nine years he'd developed the habit of holding himself aloof from all but a few persons.

His acquaintance with Lady Miranda Peverel dated from her first season, when he had been the most notable—and disinterested—of her admirers. The others had faded into the background after the Countess of Swanborough's display in Bath, but Damon had not abandoned his fair friend. He knew what it was to live in the dark shadow cast by a parent's reputation. His father, after a career as a man about town, had been a faithless and tyrannical husband, and notorious for his cruelty to both wife and child.

During his homeward walk, he reviewed his exchange with Miranda. He absolved her of any design to wrest a proposal from his reluctant lips, but she was an astute young woman and must therefore be fully aware of her aunt's ambition to see her become Lady Elston. Damon had never given anyone, least of all the duchess, cause to suppose this would ever come to pass, and it was with a free conscience that he tried to think of some other fellow who might be worthy of such a prize. Miranda was beautiful and clever, well-born and amply dowered, and no one, knowing her, could suspect her of being tainted by her mother's malady. His affection for her was strong, dating back to the time she had been a merry, lively seventeen-year-old, and signs of her former self could still be found in the wistful young woman he had just left. He was resolved to do everything in his power to smooth her path to the respectable married future she aspired to.

His brisk, purposeful stride soon brought him to Charles Street, then to the square and up the steps of Elston House. Mimms, his butler, met him at the door with the welcome news that Lord Cavender had arrived. Damon found his relative in the library, his brown head bent over the *London Gazette*. He removed his reading spectacles, revealing a face more mature than Damon remembered, and leaner. But the singular charm of Justin's smile was unaltered, as was the twinkle in his eyes.

"And now you're a viscount," Damon said when at last they were seated before the hissing fire, wineglasses in hand. "Does that mean I can't bully you as I did when you were a mere Mr. Blythe?"

"I doubt if I could be so easily bullied as I was in the days when I was mere Mr. Blythe," Justin said with a grin.

"So do I. You're rather more formidable than you used to be, but I don't think the title has much to do with it."

"I expect it comes from having worked all this time *you've* been gadding about London."

"Was playing bear-leader to a cub of a Russian prince such a hardship?" Damon retorted.

Justin shook his head. "That was a labour of love. But it happens that I was also busy with weightier duties, and I come to you direct from the Foreign Office, where I tendered the most recent—and the last—of my intelligence reports."

"Will wonders never cease," Damon murmured. "The honourable Justin a spy! I wondered why you should've stayed abroad after Lord Granville and his staff came home."

"Oh, I liked Russia well enough, never doubt it. Even after Ram died and I succeeded to my admittedly empty title, I couldn't discover that my presence or absence made much difference to anyone in England."

"Now that you're back where you belong, have you formed any precise plans?"

"So eager to be rid of me? You needn't worry, coz, I require a bed only for the night. Tomorrow I hasten to Bath."

Damon shook his head, saying firmly, "That I cannot permit—not yet. Yes, yes, I know of your mother's claim upon you, but the Duchess of Solway is giving a ball—it's her niece's birthday. I was commanded to bring you, so you must put off your journey for another day."

Justin gave him a triumphant smile. "My evening gear is probably still sitting on Yarmouth docks, a most convenient excuse for declining the invitation. The only trunk I have with me contains necessities and a few offerings for her ladyship, nothing more."

"We'll contrive something if the rest of your luggage fails to arrive in time." In Damon's mind, the issue was settled.

"I warn you, I haven't the means nor inclination to figure amongst your set," Justin declared. "I'll take my seat in the House of Lords, but socially I will remain a nonentity. I've decided to devote my energies to diplomacy and have set my sights on a place in the Foreign Office."

"I won't insist that you join in my pursuits, but you cannot hire some dismal lodging like the one you had in Lincoln's Inn. I was in fear of my life every time I climbed that rickety staircase! At the very least you must permit me to house you."

This brought a smile back to Justin's face. "What a selfish rogue you are. I'll give you my answer when I return from Bath, for I can form no decision until I've seen my mother. *And* the family solicitor," he added on a grimmer note. "I have no very clear notion of my financial state, or what debts my brother may have left."

As Damon reached for the decanter, he asked, "Do you plan to stop and see your cousin Blythe as you pass through Wiltshire?"

"Certainly. I must make the acquaintance of his son and heir."

"A hearty little rascal, by all accounts. I've not laid eyes on him since the christening."

"Do you never see Nick and Nerissa?" Justin enquired.

"They come to town once in a great while. Her ladyship is as stunning as ever, and her husband unbearably smug. No, that's not fair—he's simply content, and not ashamed of letting it be known. He writes often and lyrically about his agricultural triumphs in the hope of instilling me with a similar enthusiasm, but I ignore his less-than-subtle hints that I should interest myself in Elston Towers."

"I'm glad Nick's happy. He deserves to be, after everything he suffered at Ramsey's hands." Fixing his brown eyes on the dregs in his glass, Justin asked, "Do people still talk of the duel? Or of my brother's part in it?"

However reluctant to cause pain, Damon had to tell the truth; his cousin would accept nothing less. "Last year the tale was resurrected. There was speculation that the accident was nothing short of a suicide, although those of us who knew Ram well agree that he cared too much for his horses to willfully endanger one of them, however little he might value his own neck. I don't doubt he was riding recklessly that day, but I can't accept that he was chasing death. He spent his last years as an outcast, but I believe he was reasonably content. He had friends in his corner of Leicestershire—sporting squires and local farmers who were pleased to have a nobleman in their midst. And Uncle Isaac settled enough money on him to provide him with hunters and permit him to keep a good cellar. He never cared for much beyond that, you know."

"And that," said Justin sadly, "was the real tragedy of my brother's life."

During his years in St. Petersburg and Moscow, Justin had frequented residences far more opulent than Solway House. Even so, the ballroom commanded his admiration, and his jaded eyes approved the simple symmetry of the marble columns and were dazzled by the glittering cut-glass chandeliers which illuminated the scene.

This was the first English ball he had attended; as a young man he had been too poor and insignificant to move in the same exalted circles as his cousin. And although he was again on native soil, he felt very much the outsider, for he knew no one and was himself a complete unknown.

Standing a little apart from the company, he sipped champagne and counted the differences between this gathering and those he had frequented abroad. His countrymen's evening attire was refreshing in its plainness; foreign noblemen, most of whom held some civil or military office, wore their dress uniforms, and he was accustomed to seeing richly embroidered coats, gold and silver braid, epaulettes and jewel-encrusted orders. A rainbow of light silk gowns paraded before him, far prettier than the heavier velvets worn by Russian ladies, who also differed from their English counterparts in the display of gemstones. Here and there diamonds flashed upon bare flesh, but the majority of the Marchants' female guests wore garnets or pearls.

The young lady in whose honour this elegant company had assembled wore a white gown ornamented with silver lace, its draped bodice revealing no more of her bosom than was seemly for a lady yet unwed. Lady Miranda Peverel did not sport the ringlets favoured by so many damsels, a fashion which suddenly seemed insipid to him. Her hair was braided, and the shining black mass was bound by a pearl-studded fillet.

She was conversing with Damon in an alcove nearby, her small head tipped upward as she laughed at some remark he had made. They made an attractive couple, and their obvious and easy camaraderie caused Justin to suspect that their friendship might be one of substance, and not merely another of Damon's trifling flirtations. Lady Miranda had a history of attaching the gentlemen of his family. Lord Elston might be her suitor now, but the previous Viscount Cavender had also paid her court, before his public disgrace had sent him into exile.

Her uncle, the Duke of Solway, was not as stout as he had been three years ago; time had diminished him. His duchess was a great beauty still, her majestic person draped in apricot satin. She was circulating amongst her guests, and paused at Justin's side to say, "I'm glad Elston brought you this evening. We were so pleased to hear of your return." Although he well knew she meant to say that the duke joined in her pleasure, her regal turn of phrase reminded him of her Stuart blood, of which she was said to be very proud. With a little shake of her aristocratic head, she asked, "How could you bear to stay away for such a considerable period?"

Justin couldn't decide whether she intended this as a criticism, but just in case, he smiled disarmingly as he replied, "Russia is a wonderful, terrible country, your grace, but I'm heartily glad to be in England again."

His patriotic reply evidently pleased her, for she smiled and said, "I hope we'll often have the opportunity of seeing you at Solway House, my lord." Before moving on to speak to another of the guests crowding her ballroom, she bade him convey her warmest greetings to Lady Cavender.

Lady Miranda had left Damon's side, Justin discovered when he glanced back towards the alcove. It seemed an opportune moment to offer his felicitations, and he approached her just as the musicians began tuning their instruments.

The young lady thanked him, and he heard the trace of a laugh in her voice when she added, "But I rather think condolences are my due, Lord Cavender. Were I a gentleman, I should accept your good wishes with equanimity, but for a female twenty-one is a most daunting age! I tried to dissuade my aunt from thus exposing me, but as you can see I didn't succeed." She struck him as being a very self-assured young woman, and with good reason. Her complexion was like finest porcelain; her eyes, brilliantly blue, were fringed by thick black lashes. "Did you know that we have a family connexion?" she asked, smiling up at him in a most bewitching way.

"I'm delighted to hear it," he said gallantly, and truthfully.

"By marriage," she elaborated. "Lady Blythe, your cousin's wife, is a distant relation of mine."

He had no opportunity to reply, for at that moment Damon came to stand beside them. "Do forgive me, Justin," he said, without sounding especially apologetic, "but I've come to claim this lady." He took hold of Miranda's gloved hand. "As I outrank all your male guests, mine is the great privilege of leading you out for the first dance."

"So it is," Miranda agreed before turning to Justin. "Later, perhaps, we will be able to continue our conversation, my lord. I should so much like to hear about Russia." With a parting smile, she let Damon lead her to join the set which was forming.

As Justin watched them take their places, he supposed the young beauty would be doubly related to him before very much longer. He might have envied his kinsman that conquest, but bitter jealousy had ruled his brother's life, and he couldn't let it poison his. High time his cousin settled down and sired a pack of blue-eyed children—and the next generation of Lovells would surely be that, with such parents.

Damon and Miranda, blissfully unaware of Lord Cavender's plans for their shared future, led off the grande allemande. "Is the birthday all you hoped for, *chérie*?" he asked her.

"My expectations weren't very high to begin with, so it has easily surpassed them. To tell the truth, tonight I feel fully twice my age and entirely too old for such foolishness. I'm not eighteen this time, and it was tedious enough then."

"You haven't yet thanked me for the present I've brought," Damon murmured. "Or doesn't it take your fancy?"

"I'm at a loss to discover what you mean."

"Not what. Whom," he said pointedly. "Haven't you guessed yet? And I always judged you to be such a discerning young woman! Sweet Mira, you wanted a husband and I've already found one for you—though I admit I hadn't far to look."

Miranda missed her step. She managed to recover quickly and when the figure of the dance permitted it, she whispered, "If you're speaking of the viscount, I can only assume it's but another of your stupid jests."

"What, don't you like him?"

She failed to reply at once, but after several measures

said softly, "I'm sure Lord Cavender is a very pleasant gentleman, but I could never marry him."

"Ah, the success of my plan is now assured. Did you not know that saying 'never' is to tempt fate?"

"You are absurd," Miranda declared. "I'd marry you before I would consider your cousin, supposing either of you asked. Which," she concluded somewhat breathlessly, "is in the highest degree unlikely."

"Justin is nothing like Ram," Damon said, and for once his voice was wholly devoid of mockery. "You needn't fear that."

Miranda regarded her partner with blatant astonishment. "You are serious about this, aren't you? Oh, Damon," she sighed, "I'm sure you mean it for the best, but trust me, your attempt to set up as matchmaker won't prosper. Pray let it be a closed subject between us."

Damon bowed his golden head in assent. A moment later he noted, with intens satisfaction, that Miranda's gaze had veered off in his cousin's direction. This seemed to belie her professed indifference to a match he intended to promote with his full energies and every scrap of cunning at his disposal.

=2=

JUSTIN BLYTHE PULLED gently at the reins, and his borrowed horse came to a halt on the summit of a high ridge. As he gazed down at the house in which he'd been born eight and twenty years ago, its innumerable windows sparkled in the morning sun as if winking back a welcome.

Built of limestone yielded by local quarries, Cavender Chase was nestled in a fold of the Wiltshire downland like some rare golden ornament on a bed of green velvet. The miniature Versailles had been erected in the final decade of the seventeenth century, the joint creation of the Francophile viscount of the day and his Parisian architect. An ancient parish church sat incongruously, and in the opinion of some critics, unaesthetically close to the mansion, whose construction had so depleted the Blythe family coffers that plans for other improvements had been abandoned. Justin's grandfather and father, following the example of their ancestor, had lived expensively and well beyond their means, forever at the gaming table or on the hunting field. Their few stabs at modernisation had been sporadic at best; as a consequence, the lake, the water gardens, and the broad avenues of elm were just as they had always been. The roe deer, once raised for sport and now for show, cropped the dewy turf as they had done for generations.

On this land Justin had climbed his first tree, ridden his first pony, caught his first fish—and here the years of his boyhood had slipped away, one by one. In those long-ago days he'd been oblivious to the financial troubles that beset his mother, *de facto* steward of her improvident husband's estate. Not until after his death did she inform her younger son of the unhappy truth, that his brother would have to sell all the properties he had inherited, save one. And, Justin thought morosely, Cavender Chase might just as well have gone the way of the hunting box in Leicestershire, the sheep farm in the Cotswolds, and the manor near Newmarket, for all the good it was to him now. Before probate had been settled, Ramsey had granted a twenty-one year lease to a retired city merchant so dazzled by the magnificence of the Chase that he readily paid the exorbitant rent levied upon it. Now Ram, too, was gone, and although the property had passed to Justin, he had no right to live on it.

Disheartened, he pressed his heels into the horse's side, and it ambled down the ridge to a narrow lane that wove through arable land and meadows of grazing sheep. The sights and sounds and smells of the surrounding countryside were painfully familiar to him. With every breath he inhaled the rich aroma of rain-drenched earth, and he heard the drawn-out warble of a skylark over a fallow field. But these things failed to alleviate his sorrow; rather, they deepened it, and he wondered why he had deviated from the turnpike road. Here were too many memories of the past, and he found very little hope for the future.

The winding lane brought him to a neat brick dwelling flanked by a willow grove on one side, formal gardens on the other. The first of the family holdings to be given up, it had found a purchaser in his uncle, who had so distinguished himself in government circles that he'd been ennobled by a grateful monarch. Now his son, the second Baron Blythe, was master here. Wealthy in his own right, he had married Nerissa Newby, heiress to the vast fortune her father had acquired through trading interests, but since taking up residence at Blythe the couple had assumed a very modest style of living.

Her ladyship was presently occupied with cutting flowers, and the sound of a rider's approach caused her to look up. When she saw the horseman she let her basket and secateurs fall to the ground and hurried across the lawn. "Justin Blythe, is it *really* you? How dare you appear without the least warning!"

"I hoped you might be expecting me," he answered, reaching down to clasp the hand she held up to him.

"We have been, for a year, and had nearly given up hope of your return. Oh, how good it is to see you again—it's been an age!"

"Looking at you, Lady Blythe, I fancy it was only yesterday that we parted." This was not idle flattery, for his cousin's wife was every bit as beautiful as he remembered. Wisps of chestnut hair peeked out from beneath her broad-brimmed straw hat, and the allure of her generous mouth was heightened by a beauty mark.

"Do come into the house," she invited him. "Nick has gone to look over his potato crop and I expect him back for his tea at any moment."

"Hang Nick," Justin said merrily, "it's your son I've come to see."

"And so you shall," she responded promptly, "the minute he wakes from his rest. Did you ride over from Bath?"

"I'm on my way there now."

Shaking her head in regret, Nerissa said, "Then we cannot keep you as long as we'd like to. If you must be off soon, I'll rouse your godson at once."

"And I'll fetch your husband home. Where are these interesting potatoes to be found?"

"Just beyond our two-acre field, which lies on the other side of the hill," she said, pointing the way. "Perhaps I ought to send a groom—now we've got you back, we don't want to lose you!"

Laughing, Justin told her there was no danger of that. "I spent my youth roaming this district," he said, and with a flourish of his riding whip, he wheeled his mount around and urged it to a canter. His sinking spirits had been lifted by her ladyship's warm reception, and now he looked forward to his reunion with the baron. It took place a few minutes later, when he reached the crest of the hill and found his cousin riding directly towards him.

"Well met, farmer Nick!" he called out. "And how does your root crop prosper?"

"Very well, thank you," Lord Blythe answered, coming to a halt.

"You don't seem especially surprised to find me in Wiltshire," Justin observed. "After travelling across part of Russia and the whole of the North Sea, I had hoped for something more in the way of a greeting."

"I rather thought we might see you again this spring," Dominic replied in his distinctive, husky voice. "Nerissa met your mother in Milsom Street a fortnight ago, and she confessed her hopes. How long do you stay?"

Once again, Justin explained that he was Bath-bound. "But I couldn't pass so close to Blythe and not call."

He had last seen Dominic three years ago on the dock at Yarmouth, just before sailing away from the scandal and shame his misguided brother had brought down upon the Blythes in that fateful, fatal autumn of 1805. Smiling at his cousin, he said, "Yes, it is good to be back. A little while ago I was not so sure of it."

"Stopped at the Chase, did you?" asked the perceptive Dominic.

"Had to make sure the lawns were neatly scythed and the deer still in place." When asked if he'd gone up to the house, he confessed he had not.

"You might have done, if you wished. Your tenant is away at present."

"Is Stubbins a pleasant neighbour?" he enquired.

"I've no complaint, apart from the obvious one—he isn't you. And he's not a hunting man—but that would have bothered Ram more than it does me." Dominic's voice was slightly uneven when he spoke of the cousin who had maligned him with a vindictive lie, altering the course of both their lives, and Justin's.

"Damon sends you greetings," Justin reported.

"You've seen him?"

"I'm living with him. Elston House is my home for as long as I've need of it."

"Nerissa will be happy to know it," Dominic declared. "She worries that Damon is lonely."

"Certainly not by my definition of the word." Justin wagged his head back and forth in bemusement. "He spends no more than six hours out of the twenty-four in Berkeley Square. Your lady wastes her compassion on one who has all the advantages of wealth, property, and the leisure to enjoy them." Hearing himself, he had to ask, "Do I sound hopelessly envious?"

"You've no cause for it. I have yet to be convinced that Damon is entirely happy, and Nerissa regards him as a lost soul. She may well be right. If you're going to envy someone, it ought to be me."

"Oh, I *do*," Justin said heavily. "If you knew how much—but I won't bore you with the details of my harrowing interview with my solicitor."

"Come now, your affairs can't be as bad as all that."

"They're bad enough, as I discovered yesterday. Gregson did what he could to soften the blow, but his report on my financial state was disturbing nonetheless." Justin's long fingers tightened on the reins convulsively, and he made no attempt to conceal his desperation when he said, "If only I could be rid of those blasted mortgages! I haven't got enough capital to redeem them, and no self-respecting money-lender would grant me a shilling with my only collateral already so encumbered by debt. I suppose I might put my title on the marriage market, but I confess, Nick, I don't much fancy selling myself off to the highest bidder."

"What became of your Russian widow?" Dominic asked him. "Nerissa once laid a bet with me that you'd bring her back as your wife."

Forcing a laugh, Justin replied, "It's time to collect your winnings, and I hope I've helped you into a tidy sum. Princess Levaskov would have accepted my proposal, had I made one. As to why I didn't . . . well, you know what it means to live in exile, Nick."

"Yes," the other man said quietly, "I do know."

"I could no more ask Natasha to leave Russia than I could bear to remain there myself, so I judged it wiser to make a clean break. She claims she's eager to visit England, but her responsibilities are such that I doubt it will ever come to pass."

When they reached the house, a groom took charge of their horses and Dominic showed his visitor to the drawing-room. Lady Blythe and her young son had witnessed their approach from the window-seat, and the child ran forward to greet the baron, who said proudly, "Lord Cavender, allow me to present the Honourable Richard Sebastian Blythe."

"But because you are his godpapa," Nerissa declared, "I don't think he'll object if you call him Dickon, as we do."

Justin, whose experience with Prince Ivan Levaskov had bred in him an easy rapport with infants, gathered Dickon into his arms and lifted him high. The boy had his father's glossy black curls and his mother's blue eyes and reminded Justin of someone else with that combination of features. Setting his godson back on the floor, he turned to Nerissa. "Two nights ago I met a cousin of yours, at Solway House."

"You attended Mira's ball?" she asked, and Justin affirmed it with a nod. After she had catapulted him with eager questions about who had been present, which he answered to the best of his ability, she heaved a sigh. "I do wish I might have been there."

Her husband said wryly, "Oh? I wonder you never said as much to me."

She gave him a saucy smile. "I should hope I know better than to drag you away from your sheep and turnips and hay fields, my lord! And I doubt my presence would have benefitted Mira in any way. I'm sure she'll have a splendid success this Season, to make up for what happened after her come-out, when everyone was talking about her mother."

"That would have been after I left for Russia," Justin

mused. "Apart from the fact that Ramsey once wished to marry your cousin, I know nothing about her *or* her mother. Should I?"

"Lady Hermia Marchant, the duke's sister, was wed to the Earl of Swanborough—you know, the one with the hounds."

"My father sometimes hunted with the Swanborough Abbey pack," Justin recalled. "So did Ram."

"For a long time the Swanboroughs were childless," Nerissa continued. "Cousin Hermia was at least thirty when Mira was born, and eleven years went by before there was a male heir. The last confinement was a difficult one, no doubt because of her age, and afterwards—" Breaking off, she looked to her husband for assistance.

"Her ladyship's mind was never quite the same," Dominic elaborated.

"Swanborough sent her to Bath," said Nerissa, picking up the story. "He died the following year—of a broken heart it was said, though I don't believe it myself—and little Ninian succeeded to the earldom when he was Dickon's age." The young mother smiled at her lively son, whose sturdy legs pumped hard beneath his long skirts as he toddled about the room. When he knelt down to inspect the toes of his godfather's riding boots, Nerissa said, "The children were raised at Haberdine as wards of the duke. The year Mira turned eighteen, the duchess presented her at Court, and for several weeks she was the most admired young lady in town. But Lady Swanborough's condition had deteriorated more than anyone guessed, and that spring she created a frightful disturbance in a Bath shop. Once it became widely known, it ruined my cousin's chances for a brilliant marriage . . . or any marriage at all. She returned to Northamptonshire and has lived there quietly ever since."

Justin commented, "It is a great shame that she should have suffered so much from a scandal that was none of her making."

"Indeed," she sighed, "I've always thought it most unfair." Meeting her husband's eyes, she gave him a sad smile. "But as we have learned from experience, the world is an intolerant place."

Justin's most memorable visit to Bath had been when his mother had taken him to the Abbey to be confirmed by the Bishop of Bath and Wells. He was familiar with the city of graceful crescents and elegant parades and found it unchanged, although not as crowded as in its heyday as a watering place. His horse laboured valiantly up the steep approach to Camden Place, a classical curved row of houses that sat atop a lofty eminence.

A dark-eyed Indian manservant admitted Justin to Mr. Meriden's house. Handing over his gloves, hat, and riding whip, he said gaily, "Well, Sankar, here I am."

The Indian inclined his head respectfully. "My lord, the master and her ladyship await you. Please to follow me."

The parlour bore testimony to Mr. Isaac Meriden's long residence in the East, but many of its furnishings were new, undoubtedly the finest that a nabob's riches could procure. The room was occupied by an elderly gentleman and a silver-haired lady wearing lilac silk and a handsome shawl, who rose from the sofa. In a voice choked with tears she cried, "Dear Justin, home at last!"

He embraced her, bending down to press a tender kiss upon a cheekbone as sharply defined as his own. "Matushka," he said in teasing reproof, "if you weep all over me, I'm off on the next tide, I swear it."

This made her laugh, albeit shakily. "I'll try not to. But how *thin* you are, and ever so much taller than I remember!" She lovingly brushed away a speck of dust clinging to his lapel, then wrinkled her nose expressively. "You smell of horses. Never say you've ridden from London."

"I abandoned the mail-coach and my luggage at Calne and hired a horse at the White Hart."

"You came on the mail?" His mother echoed in dismay. "Then you haven't even slept!"

"Oh, but I did," he assured her before addressing his uncle, who had remained seated during this exchange.

"I hope to hear that Bath's famed waters have worked their magic upon you, sir."

"Not quickly enough to suit me," said Isaac Meriden gruffly. "You'll have to pardon my failure to rise; a flare-up of my gout prevents it. Take a chair, m'boy, make yourself comfortable. Alicia, pour out a cup of tea for him . . . or will you have claret instead? The doctor has forbidden me to partake of it, so I daren't join you, but you need not abstain on my account."

Justin stated his preference for tea, and Lady Cavender went to a carved sandalwood table inlaid with ebony and mother-of-pearl and busied herself with the silver urn and other tea things. She had never been a beauty, having too narrow a face and an overlong nose, but her appearance was much improved from what it once had been. Her son, remembering the shabby, outmoded gowns she'd worn during the long years of penny pinching, thought she looked very well.

"Were you able to meet with Mr. Gregson while in London?" she enquired anxiously, but Mr. Meriden drowned out his reply by asking where he'd lodged.

"With my cousin Damon," he answered, accepting a cup from his mother's hand.

For the next half hour his relations tossed out bits of news. Prices were high, consols were steady, and the royal family were held in low esteem, the result of the Duke of York's trial in the House of Commons.

"But what of yourselves?" Justin said at last. "Are you satisfied with Bath? Do you mean to make it your home?"

"Oh, aye," Mr. Meriden replied on a distinctly regretful sigh. "I've quite given up any hope of returning to Leicestershire and have sold my place. My hunting days are done, and I'm not allowed enough wine or brandy to drown my sorrow over it. Growing old is a tedious business. The day when they'll finally put me to bed with a shovel is not far off, I fear."

"Now, brother, let's not sully this happy occasion with dismal reflexions," Lady Cavender reproved him gently. After explaining to her son that Bath was rather quiet at present, she added cheerfully, "But Mrs. Jordan is playing at the Theatre Royal, and we can make up a party to go see her if you wish. When must you leave us?"

Justin placed his empty teacup on the elegant marquetry table beside his chair. "I'm entirely at your disposal, Matushka. Eventually I must return to town and take my oath in the House of Lords. Two peers of the same degree as myself must introduce me, so Damon is combing his acquaintance for a pair of willing viscounts."

"You must certainly visit Cavender Chase. I count it a stroke of good fortune that you should come back to England just when Mr. Stubbins is ready to give it up!"

"Is he? Odd that Gregson neglected to inform me."

"Oh, but he doesn't know it yet," her ladyship said blithely, "for it was only yesterday that we learned Mr. Stubbins's plans. He's in Bath and visits the Pump Room at the same hour as your uncle. Now that he has married off both his daughters, he's become sadly moped living in that great place all alone. Really, it's no wonder he began to fancy himself in poor health. And a very good thing for you that he did, if it means an end to that iniquitous lease."

It was obvious to Justin that his fond parent cherished hopes of his taking up residence at Cavender Chase, and he regretted the necessity of shattering her illusions. "A new tenant must be found, Matushka. I simply cannot afford to live there myself."

Lady Cavender and her brother exchanged a glance which spoke volumes of complicity. "Well, we shall see," she said airily. "Now, my dear, if you will excuse me, I must send a groom to fetch your luggage from the White Hart."

Her eagerness to leave the two gentlemen together on the heels of a financial discussion raised Justin's suspicions.

Mr. Meriden had returned to England over a decade ago to find his widowed sister in dire financial straits. Not only had he offered her a home, he'd granted her a generous annuity, and lacking a son to inherit his substantial fortune, he had designated her son Ramsey as his heir. But his largesse did not come without a price, and Justin was aware that the strong-willed gentleman expected the objects of his charity to bow to his every whim. Although he had no desire to be similarly beholden, Justin made up his mind to listen to whatever his uncle wished to say, no matter the cost to his pride. But he would agree to nothing.

Isaac Meriden shifted in his chair, and when he had achieved a more comfortable position, he commented, "You're not much like your brother."

"No one has ever said so. I believe Ram took after our father."

"Well, between you and me and the fire-tongs, that wasn't much to his credit. A selfish fellow, Cavender, going into debt just to keep himself in racehorses and hunters, without a care for how his boy and Alicia were going to manage after he was gone. Ram had his faults, but at least he satisfied the creditors and held on to Cavender Chase, which can't have been an easy thing. Leased his principal seat to a damned cit, but he kept it in the family." The old gentleman paused and a frown settled upon his sallow countenance. "Once, when your brother's fortunes were at low ebb, I advised him to repair them through marriage. I wonder if you would be willing to do the same."

"That solution has already suggested itself to me, sir," Justin admitted. "Are heiresses growing so thick upon the ground these days? That was not the case when I left England."

"I don't propose that you go hunting an heiress," his uncle said testily. "I already have a lady in mind, and if you agree to have her, you may trust me to make it worth your while."

"With all due respect, sir, if I were to enter into an arranged match I would prefer a bride whose family has political connexions."

The nabob smiled. "I'm no gamester, but I'd stake my last farthing on the likelihood that the Duke of Solway would be willing to do what he could for you."

"Solway?" Justin repeated. "Has he an unwed daughter?"

"No, no, the Marchant girls were married years ago. I'm speaking of his niece, Lady Miranda Peverel."

The import of this statement momentarily deprived Justin of speech.

"A charming creature," his uncle continued, "with a pleasant disposition, who'd make an ideal wife for a rising young politician. Don't smile at me for boasting of her—you'll find she outdistances my praise. You won't be disappointed, Justin, unless you're above being pleased by perfection."

Justin kept to himself the fact that he'd already met the lady and was very far from being disappointed. "But I don't aspire to perfection, sir."

Mr. Meriden hastened to point out another advantage. "Lady Mira has at least forty thousand pounds of her own, and the duke told me once he'd settled another ten on her."

Justin let his brimming amusement escape in a laugh. "Fifty thousand—and you said your candidate was no heiress! What makes you think this well-endowed female would consider a fellow who brings nothing at all into marriage?"

"There's the title. And Cavender Chase."

Justin said soberly, "If she'd wanted either, she could have wed my brother."

"I don't wish to be reminded of that business." Mr. Meriden spoke so softly that Justin scarcely caught the words. "If I'd known of Ram's involvement in Nick Blythe's duel . . . but I didn't."

He was looking grim, and Justin, thinking to please him, said he need not despair of seeing one of his nephews wed to Lady Miranda Peverel. "It is likely to happen sooner than you think, Uncle, and without my cooperation. I believe Damon is on the point of succeeding where I should undoubtedly fail."

"You think Elston is your rival?" Mr. Meriden let out a snort. "Impossible! He could've wed Lady Mira any time these three years, but he has not—and will not. It's common knowledge that the Marchants have begun looking 'round. Why else would the Duchess of Solway hasten her niece to town for the Season?"

"I'm sure I don't know, sir."

Mr. Meriden's bushy brows drew together until they met over his nose. "If the lass has a flaw, it's that she resembles her mother in more than having a name from Shakespeare. That's the custom of their family, you know. People still remember the stir Lady Hermia Marchant created in her day. Oh, I don't mean to imply she was so very sick back then, although she did have a habit of weeping uncontrollably . . . the least little thing would set her off. We fellows always used to carry an extra pocket-handkerchief when we went to balls." His gruff voice gentled when he said, "Niobe, we called her. I tumbled head over tail in love, and she had a care for me, too, though I was naught but a younger son and poor as a church mouse. Before I could declare my intentions, I got one of the housemaids with child and my pater thrust me into the East India service."

Justin, who had never been told the exact reason for his uncle's transportation, regarded him with an interest which was no longer merely polite.

"Five years later Lady Hermia wed Swanborough, who was past his first youth and in desperate need of an heir. The Abbey lies but a few leagues from Haberdine Castle, and she'd known him all her life. But after the marriage she became more and more unsteady, until neither her husband nor the duke could hide the truth. After the second child—the boy—was born, she came to Bath and has been here ever since, in the constant care of a physician."

This was the second time in a single morning that Justin had heard the melancholy tale of Lady Swanborough's mental decline.

"As I see it," the old man went on, "I've a certain duty to the poor lady's daughter. My first attempt to provide her with a husband failed, through no fault of my own. It would please me very much to see her wed to my heir—for that you are, now Ram is gone, though I doubt my money can command your obedience as it did his. So I've bought up the outstanding mortgages on Cavender Chase. Never fear," he said hastily, for Justin's face had turned as white as his neck-cloth, "I don't demand instant redemption."

"What, then?" Justin managed to ask through stiff lips.

"The opposite of that, if you but please me in this one thing. For I solemnly swear that on the day Lady Miranda Peverel becomes Viscountess Cavender, I'll consign those notes of yours to the flames."

=3=

WILLIAM MARCHANT, DUKE of Solway, leaned his grey head against the leather wing chair and closed his eyes against the sunlight spilling in from the window bay, shutting out the silhouetted figure of his niece, who read aloud from his favourite periodical. They were alone in his private study, a handsome room with mahogany bookcases of varied size, a large writing desk, a pair of globes, and a Nollekens bust of Mr. Pitt, in marble, for which his grace had paid one hundred guineas.

Miranda's crystalline voice was most soothing to a man suffering with the sort of headache which invariably followed a late night at the Westminster and another endless and inclusive debate in the House of Lords. When she reached the end of a lengthy essay entitled, "The High Sense of Honour," she looked up from the *Gentleman's Magazine*. "Shall I proceed to the review of the newest books?"

"No, my dear, that's enough for now. But stay, if you will. I'd like to talk with you." The duke opened his eyes and directed a searching glance at his companion. "I wish to know whether you like living in town, and you must tell me quite frankly if you had rather return to Haberdine."

She had been gazing absently out at the rooftop of the riding-house in Hyde Park and turned her head from the window. As she closed the journal in her lap, she sought a reply which would allay his concern. "We've been here but a fortnight. With the Season barely begun, it seems a trifle early for either of us to be disappointed by my lack of admirers."

"Admirers you have, and plenty of them."

"A lack of suitors, then," she amended. "But I'm busy enough. Last week Damon took me to the British Museum, and yesterday I went to watch him set out with the Four-in-Hand Club from Cavendish Square." She laughed softly. "What a quiz he looked! He wore a black-spotted cravat and a funny striped waistcoat, with a nosegay of pink geraniums. I wish you might have seen him."

"Oh, I've been privileged to view your cousin Gervase in driving rig many times."

A faint rap sounded on the closed door, and the butler who had grown old in the duke's service entered the room. "Your Grace asked not to be disturbed, but her ladyship has a visitor. His lordship waits in the green salon," Richards proclaimed in his measured tones. He presented his salver to Miranda, and she took up the white card. When she glanced at the name inscribed upon it, her look of surprise gave way to a conspicuously guarded expression.

"Now, now," said the duke, as she hesitated, "it isn't like you to be turning young Elston away." Miranda went to him and silently handed over the calling card. "Cavender? I thought he was still in Russia."

"He came to my birthday ball, don't you remember?" She had not forgotten Damon's foolishness on that night, when he had suggested his cousin as a prospective husband. Since then he had scarcely mentioned Lord Cavender, which encouraged her to believe he had merely been teasing her, but with Damon one could never be sure.

"You must certainly receive him, my dear. He's a connexion of Elston's, apart from your having known the brother."

"But I thought you wanted me to help you to write your next address to the House," Miranda said, unable to keep a faint note of desperation out of her voice.

"Plenty of time for that," the duke declared, leaving her with no recourse.

The green salon, so named for the silk damask lining the walls, had a domed ceiling painted with a depiction of gods and goddesses in the Verrio style, and she found Lord Cavender gazing up at it. His buff pantaloons and dark coat flattered his lean, attenuated figure, and his brown locks were slightly ruffled, either by the wind or his own long fingers. When he glanced around, his eyes met hers in a direct, probing glance, and she gave him a tentative smile.

"I confess I was surprised to learn you were here, my lord. I was not aware that you'd returned to town."

"I trust you're capable of sustaining the shock." His expression was sober, but she was quick to note the spark of humour in his brown eyes.

"So do I," she answered in kind, "for I carry no smelling salts."

"My reason for coming is twofold," he explained. "Lady Blythe charged me with delivering a message. I had the pleasure of seeing her on several occasions, and at our last meeting she bade me convey her apologies for being so poor a correspondent of late."

"She's been no worse than I," Miranda said, smiling. "I'll write Nerissa this very day, though I've little in the way of news. It was good of you to come, Lord Cavender, but she oughtn't to have put you to such trouble."

"Oh, I made it abundantly clear that I was eager to undertake the commission," Justin told her. "Which brings me to my other purpose. Perhaps I presume too much upon our very slight acquaintance, but I wonder if the improvement in the weather might incline you towards an outing. I have no carriage, but would you object to walking in the park?"

Miranda, unable to refuse so unexceptionable an invitation from so personable a gentleman, replied that she would be happy to accompany him and excused herself to put on a lemon-coloured pelisse and straw bonnet with matching ribbons. When she rejoined him, they set out to join the great parade of humanity to be found in Hyde Park of an afternoon. The day being fine, she and her escort met a host of carriages, riders, and pedestrians cramming their way through the Grosvenor Gate, and she raised no demur when her escort suggested they strike out across the grass rather than follow one of the crowded pathways.

"I fancied myself in Russia last week," he said conversationally as they walked together, "for who would expect an April snow in England, of all places?"

"Who indeed? Here in London it fell for hours and hours, all through the night and into the next day. Some of the drifts were half a foot deep or more. It soon melted, but the sun never showed its face for days on end. Had you a pleasant stay at Bath?"

"Yes and no," he temporised. "Certainly I was happy to be reunited with my mother, but it rained for most of my visit. Whenever there was a break in the showers, I rode out to Blythe or Cavender Chase."

"I've always heard that your estate is quite splendid. I wonder you could bear to leave it at this season." The words were no sooner out than Miranda belatedly recalled that the property was let. To cover her inadvertent slip of the tongue, she asked hastily, "Are they all well at Blythe? How fares my little godson?"

"Dickon Blythe is your godson?"

"And Damon's."

"And also mine," Justin told her. "I was abroad at the time of the christening. It took place in London, I think."

"Of a necessity. Dickon's other godfather has a famous aversion to the country, and the Blythes knew better than to ask him to travel to Wiltshire."

They shared a laugh over Lord Elston's most notable idiosyncrasy, and with that all constraint vanished.

"Damon always was a town creature," Justin said. "I've been coerced into attending the Royal Academy dinner tonight, so I'll have the opportunity to observe him in his element. He seems to have spent most of the past three years at art exhibitions and concerts and plays and balls."

"And race meetings," Miranda elaborated. "He does

venture into the countryside for those, but little else."

Bending down, Justin picked a bloom from a cluster of harebells. "Now this," he said, presenting it to her with a bow, "is precisely why I was so desperate to return to England. Despite the recent fall of snow, spring is more advanced than it will be in Russia."

As they moved on, Miranda told him that Lord Granville Leveson-Gower and William Ponsonby were inclined to shudder whenever they were reminded of their residence in that country.

Justin laughed. "I imagine they would do! Granville found his duties as ambassador tedious in the extreme, and he was hardly in England before the government sent him back again. And," he said, lowering his voice to a confidential murmur, "he had a narrow escape from a Russian lady who was so eager to wed him that she contemplated divorcing her husband. As for young Ponsonby, I can't imagine what complaint he might have. He lived as high as a coach horse while in Russia, sleeping till midday and seldom bestirring himself to do much of anything, which tried poor Granville's patience mightily!"

"Russia must be vastly different from England," Miranda ventured.

"Quite, yet I learned to love it. The common people are highly superstitious and sometimes seem hopelessly backward, but in general they are so good-natured that I found it easy to make allowances. I soon felt at home there, especially in Moscow. The most beautiful sight in this world must be from the height of Swallow Hill—the view of towers and church spires and at least a hundred gilded domes all shining in the sun is breathtaking. I wish you might see it!" he declared fervently.

"So do I," Miranda said.

He looked down at her and laughed, as if amused by his own enthusiasm. "One thing I don't miss is the tedious business of travelling in that country—the distances are so great! Coaches are fitted with beds, because sleeping in the carriage is usually preferable to seeking the shelter of what passes for an inn in that country, often a peasant's house, which is invariably dirty and uncomfortable. In winter the body of the coach must be removed from the wheels and drawn upon a sledge. I can't begin to describe the difficulties involved."

"It all sounds very exciting to me," Miranda confessed. "Whenever we have snow in England, everyone remains indoors, huddled at the fireside."

"And if you move so much as a foot away from the hearth, you might as well *be* outdoors," he said, and she nodded. "In Russia each room has its stove which diffuses the heat wonderfully. I never felt a draft in any of the houses I visited."

Miranda was enjoying his lordship's company and conversation so much that she failed to realise how far they'd walked until they reached the Serpentine. The viscount, she mused, was entirely different from his cousin the marquis. Damon was a many-faceted diamond, beautiful and brilliant and sharp, but his practised gallantries and endless quizzing could be tiresome. Lord Cavender's unstudied politeness and easy-going manner were more to her taste, and she felt comfortable with him. He did have one thing in common with Damon, however: he seemed to keep a part of himself closed off. But Miranda, possessing a similar reserve, could not fault him for that.

After they turned back she questioned him about Russian amusements, and when he'd described fairs and feast days, he spoke of the excellence of Moscow's actors. "Do you enjoy going to the play?" he asked her.

"Indeed I do," she answered. "But Drury Lane and Covent Garden have both burned down, and my uncle chose not to hire a box this season. He feared the quality of production might have suffered the removal to temporary quarters."

"My cousin, a regular and discriminating play-goer, has visited the Lyceum Theatre and gives a favourable report of the Drury Lane Company. He enjoined me to assist him in making up a theatre party, and I wonder if you and the duchess would consent to be a part of it. And the duke, if he wishes."

Miranda was a little troubled by this speech, for it warned that her meddlesome friend was still intent upon matchmaking. But she had too few acquaintances in town to spurn even one, and she fancied that Lord Cavender, having been so long out of England, was in a similar state. "That would be most agreeable," she answered, smiling up at him, "if Lord Elston's party falls on a night when we are not otherwise engaged."

After a thorough examination of the paintings which lined the walls of Sir George Beaumont's house, Justin gave Damon his assessment. "Our host's collection is vast enough to rival the current exhibition at the Royal Academy!"

Said his cousin, with a lazy smile, "Our host is a patron of that august body and prides himself on being a connoisseur."

The art-loving baronet had invited the cousins to a select dinner party for the Duke of York, and it was a prestigious group which had assembled in his Grosvenor Square mansion. In addition to many noblemen, several members of the Cabinet were present, including Mr. Canning and Lord Chatham. The guest of honour, His Majesty's second son, had been indicted and tried earlier in the year on the charge of profiting from the sale of army commissions, although it was his former mistress who had dirtied her hands with the illegal transactions. Damning though Mrs. Clarke's testimony had been, His Royal Highness was acquitted of any misdeeds, and no sooner had the Parliamentary enquiry concluded than he'd voluntarily resigned as commander-in-chief. The unwholesome air of scandal still clung to his large person.

A little while after Justin had been formally presented to the Duke of York, he was noticed by the foreign secretary, in his eyes a far more illustrious personage. Mr. Canning complimented him on his last report on Russian affairs before saying, "I have often heard Lord Granville commend your abilities, Lord Cavender."

"That is most gratifying, sir, but I can't think what I've ever done to merit his lordship's good opinion," Justin replied. "Having undergone several months' study at Lincoln's Inn prior to my tenure at the embassy, I confess that I did not find my duties as his scrivener especially arduous."

"So you were at Lincoln's Inn. So was I. And before that?"

"Oxford. And Eton."

"My own path exactly," Mr. Canning said with an approving nod. His right eyebrow, thinner than the left one, was oddly arched; the most prominent feature in his haughty face was his long nose. "And do you also aspire to the political life?" he asked.

"I do," said Justin frankly. "But whether I've any talent for it has yet to be proved."

"Don't be so sure. Your maiden speech in the House was received favourably by both Government and Opposition—a rare thing, as I'm sure you know. I rather think a secretarial post is beneath your touch nowadays, but there may be other possibilities. You must call upon me in Bruton Street, my lord, and we will discuss the matter at our leisure."

Justin, realising that this was no idle overture, made it clear that he would avail himself of this opportunity. The Duke of Portland was known to be in ill health, giving rise to rumours that George Canning would be the next prime minister, and anyone clinging to his coattails might be borne along to the loftiest heights imaginable.

These giddy thoughts were echoed by Damon later that evening, as they walked back to Elston House. "But," he said, "I confess I'm much less interested in your political advancement than I am in your matrimonial prospects." Justin's sudden frown was not lost upon him, and he continued. "I decided to pair you with the admired Miranda whole days before Uncle Isaac proposed her to you, and when your engagement is announced, I will demand the credit that is my due."

"I ought never have told you what transpired in Bath,"

Justin said through gritted teeth. "Let me remind you that I am by no means certain that I shall oblige our uncle."

"But you're only human, and therefore not beyond temptation. Being rid of those mortgages is no small thing, dear coz, to say nothing of the Marchant connexion. Mira has brightened your prospects like a most auspicious star, and if you fail to court her now you may well regret it later."

"Nevertheless, the thought of marrying solely for reasons of personal gain is abhorrent to me."

"That hasn't kept you away from Solway House," Damon observed shrewdly. "I understand that the lady has consented to join us at the Lyceum tomorrow evening. Evidently she finds nothing displeasing in your suit."

"You know, Damon, if you'd leave me to manage my own affairs, I should be much easier in my mind."

"Very well," he said handsomely. "I vow to keep mum as an oyster."

"I only hope you'll also be as inactive as one," his cousin retorted.

Flinging back his golden head, Damon let out a long, appreciative laugh which drowned out the cry of a passing watchman.

Miranda stepped out of the glass-walled conservatory and into the formal gardens behind her uncle's house. Drawing a deep breath, she discovered that the morning air was scented with smoke, a lingering effect of the fire which had swept through Billingsgate in the night. According to the very thorough account in the *London Gazette*, the damage to the waterfront buildings and public houses in Ralph's Quay had been great, and several docked ships bearing such highly flammable substances as oil, hemp, turpentine, and tallow were completely destroyed. Miraculously, as it seemed to her, no lives had been lost in the great conflagration.

The Solway House grounds, extensive by London standards, had lately been improved by the celebrated Mr.

Nichol, who had incorporated a fish pond and a marble fountain into the new landscape design. Miranda much preferred the old familiar avenue of yew, and followed it to her favourite bench beneath the laburnum. As she sat down in the cool shadow of the drooping branches, she was conscious of the depression which had been building gradually ever since she'd come to London.

As yet she had made no conquest, nor had any of the highly eligible gentlemen she'd met made an impression on her mind or heart.

Her aunt had pinned her hopes of the Marquis of Hartington, heir to the Duke of Devonshire. The Cavendishes were Whigs, the Marchants staunch supporters of the Government party, but political differences would never be permitted to stand in the way of so advantageous a match. His lordship was nineteen and a student at Cambridge, but he frequently abandoned his studies to attend the London balls, where he flirted with all the prettiest ladies. Though one of Miranda's favourite partners for dancing, the difference in their ages seemed much greater than two years, and she doubted he was thinking of marriage. At present he was beset by a variety of family troubles, foremost among them the question of whether his father the duke would wed Lady Elizabeth Foster, his established mistress.

Lord Granville Leveson-Gower was rumoured to be looking out for a wife. In his middle thirties, he had the reputation of being fickle, and in recent years had spurned Lady Hester Stanhope, then the Russian princess who had received his attentions during his residence in St. Petersburg, and more recently the lovely Miss Susan Beckford, a great heiress. If these ladies had failed to please him, Miranda could not imagine that she would do so. Handsome though he was, she'd struck him from her list upon hearing a rumour that he was dangling after Lady Harriet Cavendish, Lord Hartington's sister.

Damon, her sophisticated friend, was determined to remain a bachelor. His parents' scandalous, strife-ridden union had affected him profoundly; his aversion to wedlock was common knowledge. He had frequent, brief, and volatile *affaires* with highborn ladies, but thus far no female had inspired in him a lasting passion. Miranda knew him entirely too well to let herself fall in love with him. Nor could she look to any of her relations to assist her into matrimony. The Marchants were opposed to cousin marriages on principle, and there was already a case of mental instability in the family. Haunted by her mother's illness as Miranda was, her fondness for her cousin Gervase could never develop into anything warmer. Lord Edgar, the younger son and her contemporary, was serving on Sir Arthur Wellesley's staff in the Peninsula after a disastrous career at Oxford.

It was not long before the malodorous air sent her back indoors. Her aunt was in the conservatory, trying to decide which of her prized geraniums should be placed outdoors, and because Miranda had a habit of confiding in her, she voiced her concerns about her prospects for matrimony.

"I haven't noticed that you lack for partners at the assemblies at Almack's, or at any of the private balls you've attended," the older lady said soothingly. "It's far too soon to expect any of the gentlemen you've met to declare himself, and you don't want to enter into marriage too hastily, my dear."

"Do I seem so impatient?" Miranda plucked a blossom from a gardenia bush. After inhaling the heady fragrance, she expelled her breath in a long sigh. "I almost wish my papa—or Uncle William—had arranged my marriage before I left the schoolroom. It was never my ambition to make what the world would regard as a brilliant match, for beggars can't be choosers. My husband need be no more and no less than a gentleman I can like and respect, who is also able to accept the truth of my mother's illness."

The duchess transferred her attention from the geraniums to a potted lemon tree, saying absently, "I had a note from Elston this morning, another invitation to the theatre. Should I accept or refuse?"

"Oh, don't even *speak* that fiend's name to me!" Miranda said heatedly. "I'll never forgive him for the cruel trick he played upon me, no, not ever!"

"What trick was that, Mira?"

Twirling the gardenia between her fingers, she explained how Damon had taken it into his head that she ought to marry his cousin. "He thinks he's being very sly in pitching the pair of us together. Take what happened last week, for example—it was no coincidence which accounted our attending a play called *The Wedding Day*."

The duchess waited until this outburst had subsided before saying, "It seemed to me that you and Lord Cavender got on very well."

"I'm not angry with him. I won't believe he's party to Damon's scheme, or that he has the least intention of becoming my suitor."

"I confess, Mira, I think you can do better for yourself than marrying into that family," the duchess declared. "However, Nerissa's husband is proof enough that not all the Blythe men are gamesters. If you liked the viscount, your uncle wouldn't refuse his consent. It's an ancient title, going back to the time of Henry the Eighth, and I believe the Blythes were living at Cavender Chase long before that. It's a pity the young man hasn't much in the way of fortune, but with fifty thousand pounds of your own, you won't care about that." Turning back to her lemon tree, she repeated her earlier question. "So, my dear, how must I reply to Elston's note? Do we go to the theatre or not?"

"It is a matter of supreme indifference to me," the young lady said haughtily.

Two nights later, when the town coach bearing the ducal crest conveyed Miranda and her relatives to the playhouse in the Strand, she had only herself to blame.

She had dressed to please her uncle—but no other—in a gown of pale blue sarsnet, and she wore the sapphire necklace and ear-drops he had presented to her on her birthday. She clutched a silk fan with ivory sticks and medallions painted with Chinese scenes, once the property of the mother she had not seen for a decade.

The Lyceum, now the home of the Drury Lane Company, had but lately received its licence for the production of legitimate plays; previously it had been a venue for musical entertainments and waxwork exhibitions. There were four tiers of boxes, and Lord Elston's was lofty enough to possess an excellent view of the shallow stage and sloping pit. As he assisted Miranda into the chair nearest the one occupied by his cousin, he told her the ever-popular Mrs. Jordan was absent, which accounted for the number of unfilled seats.

She sat down, prey to a strong desire to strike their host's handsome, smiling face, but accepted a playbill from Lord Cavender with a faint smile. The moment she read the title of the first piece, she silently vowed revenge upon Damon for what she considered another of his tasteless—and humourless—jokes. Last week he had invited them to see *The Wedding Day*; tonight it was to be *The Honey Moon*.

In addition to displeasing her by its title, the production utterly failed to entertain her. During the intervals she pleated and unpleated her fan and watched the flirtations taking place in the boxes across the way, nodding or shaking her head whenever Lord Cavender addressed a remark to her. After what seemed to her an interminable period, the play ended and the green curtain fell that the stage might be readied for the harlequinade.

She was half-listening to a choice bit of scandal Damon was relating to the duke and duchess when the viscount addressed her in an undertone. "I fear you did not much enjoy *The Honey Moon*, Lady Miranda."

When she glanced in his direction, she was startled to find that he had put on a pair of spectacles. They gave him a scholarly aspect but did not, she decided, detract from his good looks. "The play was too derivative," she declared, "a clumsy combination of the *Taming of the Shrew* and *Twelfth Night*, both of which are far superior."

"It was not of my choosing."

"I know." She fixed her gaze upon the decorative carving of lion, shield, and unicorn at the top of the proscenium arch. "That is, I suspected as much."

"I wish you will tell me, with that candour I so much admire, if these outings are not to your taste. I can always cry off from Damon's next invitation, and then you'd be spared."

His implied understanding of her situation told her he was cognisant of Damon's dire purpose, and she fluttered her fan in an attempt to cool her face, now warm with mortification. "Oh, dear."

"Do you dislike these outings?" he persisted.

"Not that—not exactly," she faltered. "That is, I enjoyed our walk together, but this is so much less . . . comfortable."

"Because we're so closely watched," he said, completing her thought, and she nodded. "That is easily remedied. If I can induce my cousin to let me borrow his curricle, may I have the honour of driving you to Richmond? The park can be very pleasant at this time of year."

If she turned him down, he would most likely accept it as a refusal of far more than the proposed excursion. If she agreed, it would be an admission of willingness to receive him as a suitor. She looked up to find him observing her inner struggle over the gold rims of his spectacles, and a teasing light danced in his eyes.

"What say you, Lady Miranda?" he prompted. "Am I to take your silence for consent?"

"You may," she murmured, committing herself, although precisely to what she wasn't sure. Still, it would be unwise to dismiss Lord Cavender out of hand because she was cross with Damon. She should first learn whether or not he suited her requirements for a husband.

As the curtain began to rise, the gentleman leaned towards her. She felt his warm breath on her cheek when he said, "I implore you not to regard it as prophetic, but I'm afraid tonight's afterpiece is called *The Devil to Pay*."

=4=

MIRANDA HAD MET Mr. Thomas Hope, the noted art connoisseur, but had never visited his house. When she was invited to a reception to mark the christening of the gentleman's son, she supposed Damon was responsible; Mrs. Hope was reputed to be one of his flirts. Miranda's dress, a lavender silk tunic draped over a lace petticoat, had been created especially for the occasion, and Agnes had arranged her black hair in long, loose curls. Unaccustomed to wearing so fashionable a gown, she fidgeted with the wreath of white roses in her hair until her aunt's carriage reached Duchess Street. The fact that Lord Cavender was likely to be present accounted for her lavish attire—and her nervousness.

During the past fortnight their friendship had blossomed. An afternoon drive to Richmond had been the first of many excursions, and the presence of the clever, interesting gentleman had transformed the Season's balls and *soirées* from necessary ordeals into anticipated delights. Damon, inordinately pleased with the result of his matchmaking efforts, had informed her that the issue of whether or not Lord Cavender would propose was not considered worth betting on at the gentlemen's clubs; the outcome was too certain. In common with the members of White's, she believed an offer of marriage was imminent, and with each passing day the prospect grew more agreeable.

Although she'd been prepared to settle for a marriage

of convenience, she counted it a stroke of good fortune that she had met a gentleman for whom she could feel much more than liking and respect. She'd never loved before, not in this way, and her own susceptibility surprised her. Lord Cavender had touched her heart in a few short weeks, and she believed her effect upon him was the same. Thus far he'd refrained from any display other than a friendly smile and a gentle pressure on her hand when he held it at meeting and parting, but sometimes when they were together she was conscious of a warmth in his eyes that communicated his desire to do far more.

When she walked past the impassive stone sphinxes guarding the door of Mr. Hope's residence, she experienced that agreeable fluttering of her pulse which had preceded all earlier encounters with her suitor.

A large hall decorated in the style of a Greek temple housed a part of Mr. Hope's collection of statuary, and his pretty wife was receiving her guests there. "How happy I am to see your grace," she said, "and also Lady Miranda. We have the honour of receiving the Princess of Wales this evening, and I'm sure her ladyship will wish to be presented if she has not been already."

A marked expression of disapproval flitted across the duchess's face, and as soon as they were out of earshot she commented to Miranda, "I should think a bishop's daughter would know it's no great thing, having the princess at her party. Her husband must have persuaded her it was the thing to do. I confess, I never thought much of these Hopes. Dutch bankers and merchants, the lot of them, and why they couldn't have remained in Amsterdam, I'm sure I don't know." Her grey eyes swept the room. "I see Lord Lyttelton and Lady Sheffield. Miss Berry is here with her sister. Come, we ought to speak to them."

Mary Berry had lived in society for most of her forty-six years and was therefore invited everywhere. She shared a house in Curzon Street with her sister; it had become a popular resort for the nobility, the gentry, and various literary lions. When she saw Miranda, her dark eyes snapped with lively interest, for she knew about Lord Cavender's determined pursuit.

"To be sure, his lordship is a charming gentleman, with that exotic air which comes from living in foreign places," Miss Berry declared. "But Agnes and I had quite set our hearts upon matching you with Lord Hartington. In my next letter to Cambridge I shall certainly scold our young friend for letting you slip away!"

Miranda was rescued from the spinster's quizzing by Lord Lyttelton, and while she was chatting amiably with him she heard her aunt make a low noise which sounded suspiciously like a groan. Miranda looked up to see that a circle of persons, Damon among them, was gathered around a coarse-featured lady with rouged cheeks, whose gown was cut low to display an abundance of plump, bare flesh. "She has noticed you," the duchess hissed. "Already she's asking Elston who you are. I'm afraid we cannot avoid an introduction."

Miranda's subsequent presentation was not her first encounter with royalty; she had made her curtsey to the king and queen three years before, during her first season. The Princess of Wales seldom went to Court, but despite her constant and bitter battles with her husband, she'd remained on reasonably good terms with her in-laws.

Caroline smiled when Lord Elston introduced Miranda as his friend and said, "Och, I'm sure many gentlemans vant to be her ladyship's friend, so pretty iss she!" Lifting her painted brows, she asked, "And you, Lady Miranda, haff you broken many hearts?"

However indelicate the question, it was uttered with such good humour that Miranda could not take offence. Rising from a deep curtsey, she replied, "I sincerely hope not, ma'am." This reply elicited a loud laugh from Caroline, whose cheeks resembled a pair of shiny red apples. As the marquis ushered the young lady out of her presence, she nodded at Lady Sheffield, who then brought Miss Berry forward to be presented.

Miranda accepted Damon's offer to show her over the house but told him frankly, "I can't imagine anyone living here. It is too much like a museum."

"And—the public are sometimes admitted to view Hope's collections. He's not especially popular, not even among those artists he patronises, but Louisa's a good sort. This is the vase room, his pride and joy."

Miranda dutifully admired the contents of a succession of glass cases holding, according to Damon, more than five hundred vases; many were antique, some of modern manufacture. He showed her the Indian Room and another fitted up in the Egyptian style, and lastly they reached one filled with curiosities of Hindu and Chinese worship, but she was not so distracted by the displays that she failed to note Lord Cavender's absence. "I thought I might see your cousin here," she ventured as they entered one gallery.

"He expected to be detained late at the House of Lords and begged me to make his excuses to you." Conscious of her disappointment, Damon said in a rallying voice, "A pity he won't see all your finery, but never fear, I'll make a point of telling him how ravishing you looked." He gave her a long, keen look. "Are you still angry that I brought Justin to your birthday ball?"

"I was never angry about that," she answered, smiling. "It was only those horrid nights at the theatre."

"And I was so hoping the pair of you would wish to attend the performance of *Man and Wife* this Friday! Wicked creatures, you prefer leisurely drives into the countryside—in my curricle—and uninterrupted flirtation in the groves of Kensington Gardens, don't you?"

"Is there *anything* you don't know?" she murmured, her cheeks suffused with colour. "Who spies for you?"

"Oh, Justin knows better than to keep secrets from me. Have you decided yet who will be your bridesmaids, *chérie*?"

"I don't know that I'll have need of any," she answered primly.

"You will," he said firmly. "And if you marry my

cousin, I'll kiss your foot and swear myself your subject. The hopes of so many are pinned upon you. I don't want Justin to turn into a crusty bachelor like myself. His mother also yearns to see him wed, and my uncle is mad for the marriage. He fancies he made it himself."

"What do you know of it?" she laughed.

"More than you," he retorted.

"Is Mr. Meriden in town? Have you seen him?"

"Not lately, but I expect I soon shall—at your wedding. Justin's his heir, didn't you know?" She shook her head, and he drawled, "What a singularly humble individual my cousin is, to be sure. And I suppose he also neglected to tell you that our uncle has made it possible for him to reclaim his estate." He delved into his coat pocket for his snuffbox. "Uncle Meriden holds the mortgages on Cavender Chase and has promised to forgive the remaining debt if Justin obliges him by marrying you. A handsome wedding present, wouldn't you say?"

Miranda fixed startled eyes on Damon's smiling face. "Are you sure of this?" she asked faintly.

"Justin told me himself, immediately upon his return from Bath." Her reception of this news was not what he expected; the high colour had flown from her cheeks.

"Why should Mr. Meriden choose me?"

Damon shrugged. "Does it matter? I thought you'd be pleased to know you'll be the means of restoring Justin's property to him."

"Pleased?" she choked. "Oh, Damon, how very little you know me if you could be so mistaken."

Before Damon could stop her she hurried away, and he was prevented from following by a fellow patron of the Royal Academy, who asked his opinion of a Chinese screen in the next room.

He still had not found Miranda when the dancing began, though he looked for her in every crowded room. He returned to the statue gallery to find Lord Lyttelton dancing with the Princess of Wales. The ill-matched couple galloped up and down the room, the lady's prominent bosom bobbing, her face crimson from exertion. Some of the onlookers appeared to be appalled by this exhibition, others were amused, and Damon, his attention caught, forgot Miranda's mysterious disappearance.

The monarch's seventy-first birthday fell upon the Sabbath, and the piety of the English was such that the celebrations and processions were postponed until the day after, when it rained. But the showers could not dampen the spirits of King George's subjects, and Justin passed many a drunken reveller when he walked from his cousin's house to the splendid white mansion at the corner of Mount Street and Park Lane.

He had not seen Lady Miranda Peverel for nearly a week, and although he'd attended two evening parties in the past two days in the expectation of meeting her, she had been absent from both. Damon, who had left town to attend a race meeting, reported having seen her at Mrs. Hope's *soirée* last week. Justin, wondering if she might have fallen ill, had accosted her uncle at a political dinner, and after being assured that she was in good health, asked permission to marry her.

Before meeting Lady Miranda, he had never quite accepted the idea of marriage as a means of improving his fortunes. As a younger son, he'd always been destined to enter a profession, but during his first term at Lincoln's Inn, Dominic Blythe's duel had plunged him into a courtroom, where he discovered just how unpleasant the business of practising law could be. Still, he would have held on to his clerkship had not his brother and his cousins urged him to accept the post of secretary to Lord Granville in St. Petersburg, so to Russia he had gone.

He had returned as Viscount Cavender. Now he possessed a seat in Parliament, his for life, and had placed his feet firmly upon the path to prominence. His friendship with Mr. Canning prospered, and he hoped it might lead to the desired employment at the Foreign Office.

As his uncle had pointed out, and as he had lately discovered for himself, Lady Miranda would be the perfect wife for a gentleman with aspirations to a diplomatic post.

Her lineage was impeccable, her fortune was immense, and her family's politics agreed with his own. She was also charming and lovely and would, Justin believed, make an excellent chatelaine of Cavender Chase. That was an important consideration, for if all went according to plan, he would someday be posted to some foreign land as an emissary, perhaps even as ambassador.

The footman who admitted him to Solway House warned him that her ladyship might not be at home to visitors, but he said confidently, "Tell her I've come on a matter of some importance."

It seemed a very long time before Lady Miranda stepped into the salon, dressed in her riding habit. To Justin's eyes she looked pale and uneasy, and he asked if she'd received bad news.

"No—oh, no," she said, and gave a hollow little laugh in which he detected not a jot of genuine mirth. "I'm occasionally prone to low moods, but they soon pass."

Justin could see that it was not the most propitious time to embark upon the business which had brought him. "Perhaps I will be able to cheer you," he ventured, but his smile went unanswered. Her manner was so strange that he wondered if the duke had broken his promise of silence and told her of their brief discussion. But surely that would not make her look so desperately unhappy; she had received his attentions with every sign of delight.

"Lady Miranda, you must be aware of certain rumours about my intentions towards you," he began, and she bowed her head. "They are entirely founded upon truth. Does that displease you?" he asked gently.

Her black head jerked upward and she said hastily, "My lord, I cannot—I must not stay. Lord Hartington is coming at half past three and. . . ." Her voice trailed off, and she gazed at him helplessly.

She had not misunderstood: he read frightened comprehension in her face. "I had all manner of pretty speeches prepared, which I will happily recite as soon as I have your answer to the question which brings me here today. It is my earnest desire to make you my wife, though we haven't known one another for very long, and I take such pleasure in your company that I hope you will say yes."

To his astonishment, large tears began to slide down her cheeks. "Lord Cavender, I am very sorry if I have given you any cause to believe that we can be anything more than—than what we are now. You do me great honour, but I cannot marry you."

With her first apologetic words his mouth and throat had gone dry, but he swiftly recovered from the shock and said, "If you feel this is too sudden, too soon, I do understand. Only tell me that I need not despair of succeeding after we know one another better."

"I can hold out no such hope, my lord."

He thought her voice carried a faint note of regret, but whether it was genuine or merely polite he could not tell. Then it occurred to him why she might have reservations about becoming Lady Cavender. "You need not doubt my ability to support you—I would not have addressed you otherwise. I laid the facts before your uncle, but you have a right to know the truth, for you are the one who will be most affected. I haven't much in the way of an inheritance. Three generations of neglect have all but ruined my estate, and my present income is somewhat limited as a result. For nigh on twenty years no Blythe has lived at Cavender Chase. Though my brother let the house on a long lease, the farms have short ones, and we've lost several good tenants. So much needs to be done to restore my property and make it profitable again, I don't deny that, but it's something I think we might do together, you and I."

"With my funds?"

"And my own hard work," he said, relieved to have some clue to the cause of her reluctance. "You must hear me out," he pleaded, covering the distance she had put between them. "My estate is heavily encumbered, but that needn't worry you. My debts will be settled in good time, I promise."

She withdrew even further. "Please say no more, Lord Cavender."

Never in his life had he felt so powerless, but he could not give up. "The esteem, the affection I feel for you—these mean nothing?"

"They would mean a great deal, if only . . ." The words seemed to fail her, and she shook her head.

"If only you could believe that I'm not a fortune-hunter," he finished for her.

None of his arguments had swayed her, and none, he realised unhappily, ever would. Her fifty thousand pounds was partly responsible for his interest in her; he would be dishonest if he denied it. To lose that which he'd been so sure of winning was difficult to accept, but consideration for her feelings demanded that he contain his dismay.

"I regret that our pleasant association should have given you any cause for pain," he told her gravely. "Please to accept my heartfelt wishes for your future happiness." He shook her hand before leaving; it trembled slightly and was small and cold against his own.

Miranda was afraid her physical symptoms—the tears, the quiver in her voice, the nervous tremour—had alerted him to the fact that she had wanted to give him another answer. In recent days she'd played out the scene in her mind to prepare herself, and never had it ended thus. She couldn't even be sure his motive had been mercenary, for he'd said everything she'd most wanted to hear, but by doing so, he had raised more questions than he'd answered.

Hearing the rustle of skirts, she looked around to see her aunt advance into the room. "Is it done?" she asked softly.

"Yes," Miranda choked, "he has gone."

"Now you may be easy," the duchess said as she smoothed the dark, drooping head tenderly.

"It will be a long time before I am that," Miranda sighed. "He sounded so sincere, I wanted to believe him. Suppose he really does care?"

"A young lady is not obliged to marry a gentleman

simply because he has a fondness for her. You, Miranda, are free to choose whomever you please when you please, and for any reason which seems best to you."

"But what if I receive no other offer?" Miranda wondered.

The Duchess of Solway smiled sympathetically. "It is a difficult business, refusing a proposal of marriage. I dimly recall my own disordered feelings on the three occasions that I performed the same unhappy task. You can except some degree of awkwardness between you and Lord Cavender. It may never disappear entirely. But your pain will pass, I promise you. Now run upstairs and wash your pretty face, my dear. The Marquis of Hartington will soon be here."

When Damon returned to London, he found the festive bunting drenched by rain; the banners proclaiming "God Save the King" were sodden and bedraggled. His curricle sped along Piccadilly in the wake of parading soldiers and a military band, his horses exhibiting a well-bred detachment as they passed the cheering public.

When he arrived at Elston House, he paused in the hall to remove his long driving coat, which covered a plain jacket and light-coloured breeches with mother-of-pearl buttons. His cravat had black spots the size of currants, and he wore a waistcoat with vertical stripes, blue alternating with canary yellow, both of which designated him a member of the prestigious Four-in-Hand Club. He did not go up to change, but entered the library. Justin was there, reading the *Times*. Making his way to the decanter he said merrily, "Hullo, coz. Care to take a glass of brandy with me?"

Justin lowered his paper, then climbed to his feet. "I'm glad you're back. I've been wanting to speak with you."

The displeasure in Justin's voice was new to Damon, and he deduced that something unpleasant had occurred in his absence. Whatever it was, he hoped it hadn't damaged his cousin's chances of employment at the Foreign Office. "You have my whole attention," he announced when he handed Justin a glass.

"If you were not a relation of mine, I would call you out over the fine trick you've served me. Did you really intend to keep her for yourself?"

After a startled moment, Damon replied, "Forgive me if I seem obtuse, but I cannot fathom whom or what you are speaking about."

"Last week, possibly at Mrs. Hope's reception, you made some comment to Lady Miranda about my being on the lookout for a rich wife. After which, you left town like a damned coward, without the slightest warning to me about what had passed between you. I only learned of it today, and in an exceedingly untimely and unfortunate fashion."

"Justin, I meant no harm by it."

"Lady Miranda has refused me, as you no doubt expected she would do. Accept my congratulations—you've managed to roll me up very neatly."

"I expected nothing of the sort," Damon protested, "though I *did* tell Mira that Uncle Isaac pointed her out to you as a suitable bride." He had said rather more but preferred to conceal that from his glowering cousin. "Was that so very wrong of me?"

"Worse than wrong," Justin shot back. "It is unforgivable!"

Damon was silent, too fascinated by this odd, highly volatile Justin to form a reply. Finally he said, "If I did you a disservice it was unintentional. I regret it no less than you do."

"Your regret is no help to me now that she's convinced I'm naught but a scheming fortune-hunter."

"Shall I go and tell her you're not?"

"It wouldn't do any good," was Justin's bitter reply. "She won't have me."

Damon smiled derisively and commented, "You are behaving suspiciously like a man disappointed in love."

"I never pretended that my feelings ran to such lengths as that. I had begun to care for her, and it might have led to something more . . . now I shall never know. If you could have seen her face when I asked her to be my wife—I'll not forget it till my dying day. She has been hurt, deeply hurt, and I've had a hand in it, however unwittingly. So have you." Justin tossed off the dregs of his brandy, turned on his heel, and left the room.

Damon, knowing even better than Justin how tender-hearted Miranda was, let fly an oath which echoed in the silent room. He couldn't recall everything he'd told her, but he'd mentioned those mortgages in addition to revealing Isaac Meriden's part in bringing the pair together. Miranda deserved to know the truth, he reassured himself, uncomfortable with his own culpability, and if she didn't like it, surely he was not to blame. And if Justin had chosen her solely for the pecuniary advantage to himself, she was far better off without him; she wasn't cut out for a cold-blooded marriage of convenience. While Damon regretted that she had suffered a disappointment, he couldn't be sorry that he'd been the means of saving his tender-hearted friend from a union which might cause her even greater unhappiness in the future.

=5=

"How PRETTY THE fleet looks when it comes in," Lord Hartington called to Miranda as he stood at the edge of a high cliff overlooking the English Channel.

"Yes, quite." She was seated in a small cart, struggling to subdue a pair of cream-coloured ponies. They had turned out to be less docile than they appeared and were as stubborn and unreliable as the donkey teams preferred by some of Brighton's lady whips. She tugged fiercely on the reins to bring the ponies to a standstill beside her fair-haired escort so she could gaze out over the water. The local fishing boats, nearly a hundred in number, had appeared on the horizon, their white sails clearly visible against the blue waters. Lost in admiration of the view, Miranda let the reins fall slack, and her team darted forward.

The Marquis of Hartington chased after her, his long legs bringing him to her rescue. "Trying to give me the slip, Lady Mira?" he quizzed her, grasping one bridle.

"Of course I wasn't," she protested, laughing. "It's only that I have no skill for driving, nor have I the patience to continue all the way to Rottingdean. Do you mind if we turn back?"

His lordship didn't mind in the least, and when he offered to lead the team for her, Miranda nodded gratefully. They proceeded without further mishap, following the path down to the beach, where the bathing machines were being drawn out of the water by plodding horses.

This, like the return of the fishing boats, was an afternoon ritual at the seaside resort.

It was unfashionably early for a visit to Brighton, but the Duchess of Solway, seeking a cure for her husband's frequent headaches and her niece's low spirits, had arrived at the end of June, in advance of the rest of society. Her hope that Miranda might attach the Duke of Devonshire's heir had not faded, so she was delighted to discover Lord Hartington there for the purpose of restoring his health after an illness.

Miranda's lively friend was desperately bored and he welcomed feminine companionship after a period of deprivation. He called upon her every day, took her driving in his curricle, and counted the days until the seasonal balls would begin at the Castle Inn and the Old Ship. He was an attractive gentleman, bright and amusing, and as accomplished a flirt as he was a dancer. At a very young age he had bestowed his affections upon his cousin, Caro Ponsonby, who had married William Lamb. Hart had not fully recovered from that disappointment when he lost his mother, to whom he had been greatly attached. Miranda didn't wish to marry him, but she also suffered from *ennui* and shattered hopes, and stood in need of diversion.

"Have you taken to the waters yet?" she asked him, but he was a trifle deaf and failed to hear, so she was obliged to repeat the question.

"I dip myself each morning, as my London physician prescribed," his lordship answered. "And you?"

"I haven't yet screwed up my courage," Miranda confessed. "The only time I ever went sea-bathing was at Scarborough, when I was very young. I didn't like it above half." During her childhood she had often accompanied her parents to spas and watering places as they sought a cure for Lady Swanborough's barrenness and melancholy. One summer they had gone to Yorkshire, staying at Harrogate and Scarborough. Miranda's brother had been born the following winter, and afterwards her mother had gone to Bath, never to return.

"When we return the cart," said Lord Hartington, "I shall certainly give that rascal a piece of my mind for foisting such stubborn, ill-natured beasts upon us!"

But he was so affable and inoffensive a fellow that his scold made little impression. After venting his spleen, Hart handed over the required sum and escorted Miranda back to the Royal Crescent, where her uncle had taken a house. The houses were uniformly faced with glazed black mathematical tiles, and each one had bow windows on the ground floor, classical doorways, and a pretty ironwork balcony above.

A life-sized statue on a massive pedestal decorated the half-moon of green lawn, and as they passed it Hart told her, "Yesterday in Donaldson's Library I overheard a gentleman tell his friend that a fine memorial to Lord Nelson could be seen in the Crescent."

"But it's meant to be the Prince of Wales!" The object under discussion had been fashioned from Coad's Artificial Stone, a plaster-like substance, and was sadly weatherbeaten. A recent storm had taken one upraised arm off at the elbow, leaving a stump. "It does look a bit like one of Lord Nelson," she conceded. "He's even facing the sea, as an admiral should." When she invited Lord Hartington to come inside, he declined, pleading an engagement to meet an acquaintance at Raggett's club. They agreed upon a time for their daily ride on the downs and parted on her doorstep.

Miranda had not objected to being uprooted from London and transplanted to sunny Brighton, for even if one chose not to go sea-bathing, the town offered a variety of amusements. She had been there but a few days and had already added her name to the list of library patrons. She had attended a card assembly at the Old Ship and a military review on the downs, and every evening she promenaded on the Steyne with her aunt and uncle. Today she had achieved her ambition of driving a pony cart. And despite all of this hectic activity, she had never forgotten Lord Cavender.

The viscount, the third member of his family to dangle

after her, was the first one she had sighed for. His hunting-mad brother had been too old for her, and his handsome cousin was too detached. Her infatuation with him should not have survived Damon's revelation concerning the motive of Justin's courtship, but it had. And shame though it was to her, she missed him. For a few joyous weeks she had felt herself worthy of a gentleman's admiration and had foolishly aspired to win his love.

Although Justin had wearied of the London social scene, he hadn't broken his habit of accepting the majority of the invitations which came his way. But he no longer attended parties in the hope of seeing Lady Miranda Peverel, nor in his cousin's company. Ever since the quarrel, they had gone their separate ways, day and night. Damon dined at his club and graced the gatherings hosted by his artistic friends, while Justin participated in debates in the House of Lords and from there went to dinners given by political leaders. When their paths crossed it was usually by chance, and although they acknowledged one another, their comradeship was a thing of the past. But Justin was not lonely; he had been taken up by Lord Granville Leveson-Gower, formerly the ambassador to Russia.

Late in June, several weeks after Justin had alienated Lady Miranda, he accompanied his friend to a formal party at a nobleman's house. The fashionable company included Lord and Lady Hinchinbroke, Mr. Pierrepoint, and most significantly Lady Harriet Cavendish, chaperoned by her sister, Lady Morpeth. For most of the evening Lord Granville avoided her and flirted with all the other ladies, and before everyone went into dinner Justin took him to task.

"Your behaviour tonight is not likely to impress Lady Harriet with anything but your lack of constancy," he said, and when Lord Granville opened his blue eyes wide, he laughed. "Did you think I hadn't noticed that you've been careful to show your face at every party she has attended this season?"

His lordship shrugged. "I confess, the lady interests me, though I'm not yet ready to slip my neck into the matrimonial noose. I can't be sure that Lady Harriet will ever regard me as anything more than her aunt's *cavalier servante*. My friendship with Lady Bessborough is of such long standing that it may prove an insuperable barrier to marriage with her niece. But it is a suitable alliance," Granville said, a note of defiance in his voice. "Our families have been intimate for many years."

"Indeed, but in such a way as to give Lady Harriet pause," Justin commented dryly.

Lord Granville glanced around to make certain there was no danger of being overheard before saying in a low voice, "Here's something you'll want to know. It won't be made public for two days, so I must trust you to keep silent." Having captured Justin's full attention, he announced, "I've been named Secretary at War and am going to sit in Cabinet."

"When the official announcement is made, I shall pretend to be very surprised and will *strive* to seem pleased," Justin assured him, his eyes dancing.

"Strive to—oh, you're joking with me, are you? Have a care, Cavender. I possess the power to make you or break you!"

"I humbly beg your lordship's forgiveness for my impudence." Placing a hand on his friend's broad shoulder, Justin congratulated him on his appointment. "It's the best news I've heard in an age!"

"I wonder whether anyone else will agree with you," Granville murmured, his eyes seeking Lady Harriet. "Do you think she will remain so disdainful after I become a Cabinet minister?" he asked plaintively.

"Who can tell? My faith in the fair sex has been altogether shattered of late, as you know. Bitter experience has left me a husk of a man."

At dinner Justin sat next to a solemn, quiet girl and would have exerted himself to draw her out had he not been monopolised by his other partner, a vivacious beauty who kept up a running commentary on the company.

"How peevish Lady Harriet looks," Miss Mellish said to him midway through the first course. "I daresay she covets her sister's place beside Lord Granville, or perhaps she's missing her brother. Well, to be sure we all do, now that he's left us."

"Has he?"

"Dr. Farquhar sent him to Brighton," said the knowledgeable young lady. "Poor Lord Hartington, he was positively chased to the seacoast, and in his weakened condition he'll make easy prey for that scheming duchess."

Justin, after a swift mental review of the latest *on-dits*, hit upon none that linked Devonshire's heir to a duchess. He let the remark pass without comment and was about to turn to the shy, blessedly silent lady on his other side when Miss Mellish addressed him once more. "Of course, she's so desperate to be rid of her niece that she'll take her chances with any likely gentleman. Why, I do believe you were encouraged to run tame at Solway House, were you not, Lord Cavender? Hart will find himself *besieged*. I despise matchmaking, don't you?" She reached for her wineglass. Justin, taking advantage of this respite to eat, discovered that his appetite was not so sharp as it had been. Nevertheless, he took up his fork and speared a stalk of asparagus savagely.

When he'd first heard about Lady Miranda's abrupt departure from town, he had accepted the tale that her uncle's health was responsible, but now Miss Mellish had presented a more disturbing possibility. Was she correct? Had the Marchants hurried to the coast to dangle the lovely Miranda before a susceptible young man who was heir to a dukedom? Justin knew it was no business of his, but he hadn't yet steeled himself to accept her inevitable engagement to another.

"Lady Mira has no hope of becoming Hart's bride," Miss Mellish declared, and he supposed she was trying to convince herself. "The Cavendishes will never permit him to wed the daughter of a woman who is out of her senses."

Justin's resentment was roused by the spiteful note

which had crept into the strident voice. Determined to champion the lady who had rejected him, he rounded on Miss Mellish. "Would our nation refuse to have the Prince of Wales as king because his father has had bouts of madness?"

"Oh, but that is entirely different," she protested.

"Is it? Take care, ma'am, or you may one day find yourself accused of treason."

The young lady shrugged one bare shoulder and turned her head to begin a conversation with the gentleman on her other side. Justin, welcoming the rebuff, devoted himself to the quiet girl for the rest of the meal, and found her far more congenial, if a trifle dull.

Later he sought out the Cavendish sisters. Although the elder had an air of distinction and the younger possessed wit and intelligence, neither Lady Morpeth nor Lady Harriet lived up to the standard of beauty set by their mother, the late Duchess of Devonshire. Of her grace's three children, it was only the youngest, Lord Hartington, who had inherited a semblance of her famed looks and charm.

Taking a chair near Lady Harriet, he said he hoped her brother's health had mended since going to Brighton.

"I had a letter today," she replied, "and can report that he's going on very well."

"Do you intend to join Lord Hartington?"

"I wish I might," she said wistfully, "I'm so tired of London. But so is everyone at the close of the Season." Her face was round and plain; the small blue eyes were expressive of unhappiness, and Justin hoped his dashing, fickle friend was not the cause of it.

"What does Lord Hartington find to amuse him, I wonder, when all of society is still to be found here?"

"I suspect his rapid recovery is due to the presence of a young lady known to us both. All night his dejected admirers have asked Georgiana and me when he'll return, but I know not."

It was not long before the party began to break up. Justin and Lord Granville left together, both preoccupied with thought as the carriage bore them along the lamplit streets.

When they approached Berkeley Square, Granville spoke up, saying crossly, "I saw how you attached yourself to Lady Harriet after supper, Justin. Are you my rival?"

"I was merely asking after her brother, who has been unwell."

Granville sighed deeply. "Was that the cause of her abstraction, do you think?"

"I don't know the lady well enough to speculate."

"Did you hear that her brother is cosying up to Mira Peveral down in Brighton? Their father is sure to marry Lady Liz Foster before long, so says Lady Bessborough. And I know Lady Harry and Lord Hart both detest their future stepmother. I daresay they'll want to form establishments of their own in preference to forming part of the duke's ménage." On a note of satisfaction, Granville concluded, "I predict that we'll see Devonshire, his son, *and* his daughter all wed by the year's end."

"Not if I can prevent it," Justin muttered under his breath.

"All the decent lodgings will be taken already," Damon commented at breakfast, when his cousin expressed the intention of travelling to Brighton.

"I plan to make use of yours," Justin announced. "Isn't it your habit to engage the same suite of rooms at the Castle Inn every year?"

"But I might wish to stay there myself!"

Justin unfolded his spectacles and said with quiet conviction, "As I see it, you owe me a favour."

Damon regarded his obdurate relative in dismay. "Where am I to go? Everyone will be leaving town within a few weeks."

"Drop a few hints, get yourself invited somewhere—anywhere but Brighton."

Damon rose and made an impatient circle around the table. "Oh, very well," he said at last, with poor grace. "Some friends plan to make a tour of the Lake District, and they did ask me to join them out of courtesy, and with no expectation that I'd accept. They know I abominate scenery, unless it's framed in gilt and hanging on a wall." He looked at Justin, who was reading a letter from Lady Cavender. "Shall I write to the proprietor of the Castle and inform him that you're to have my billet?"

"Yes, thank you."

Hoping to impress his cousin with his selflessness, and feeling the need to further atone for his sins, he said handsomely, "I'll even frank your expedition. You may charge your bed and board to my account."

"That won't be necessary," Justin replied without looking up from his letter.

"Brighton's an expensive place," Damon warned him.

"With quarter-day just past, I'm reasonably plump in the pocket."

When Damon tried to point out that it might be ruinous for him to leave London just as his sponsor was being promoted to the Cabinet, he said he was confident that if a post in the Foreign Office should suddenly open up, Granville would persuade Mr. Canning to hold it for him for a few weeks. "This new ruthlessness becomes you," Damon observed, "and most young maidens secretly long to be swept off their feet. Don't give me that guileless look. I know she's there. Do you honestly think you will succeed?"

"I have no real hope of doing so," Justin admitted. "But I assure you I'm prepared to do whatever necessary to convince her of my sincerity."

The next day he presented himself at the Golden Cross in time to board the fast coach for Brighton. He'd heard enough of his cousin's mockery to last a lifetime, but it hadn't deterred him; neither had the prospect of failure. It might be that Lady Miranda had always intended to marry Lord Hartington and had entertained other suitors only to spur him on, but he could not let her go to another man without learning if he still had a chance.

It was afternoon when he reached the seaside resort, and he made his way unerringly to the inn closest to the

Marine Pavilion. The landlord of the Castle had received the letter Lord Elston had sent by express and he showed his guest to a handsome set of apartments on an upper floor. The high, arched windows commanded a view of the Steyne, permitting Justin to spy upon the ladies walking there. A cluster of gentlemen browsed in front of Donaldson's Library across the way, and he could see the facades of four horses in the South Parade painted in the colours of the Whig party, known locally as the Blue and Buffs. Apart from the pavilion itself, which was in a constant state of renovation, the town was little changed. The same could not be said of himself. Leaning out the window to catch a glimpse of the distant ocean, he marvelled at all that had happened to him since leaving Russia, good and bad. He'd resumed his warm friendship with Granville and had attracted the notice of the foreign secretary, both of which augured well for his political future. But his relationship with Damon had altered, perhaps forever, and all because of a lady who had been a stranger to him when he had first returned to England.

=6=

"HAVE A CARE, DEARIE," the attendant cautioned when Miranda descended the wooden steps of the bathing-machine.

Her bare feet grazing the rough, flat bed of sand, she waded through the cold water until it lapped at her waist. Then she bent her knees slightly to submerge her upper body, but after a few experimental dips she simply stood there, enjoying her new perspective of the world. The white buildings of Brighton were stretched out before her, and she could trace the chalky cliffs and the sweep of the downs in the background. Her coarse brown shift, now soaked, clung to her skin, its long skirt billowing with each wave that rolled in. "This is very refreshing," she called to Agnes Bleaklow, who sat on the bench inside the box-like caravan.

As she ventured into deeper waters, her maid begged her not to wear herself out, but Miranda paid no heed. After the bathing woman had shown her how to float on the surface of the sea, she was even more reluctant to curtail her fun. Unused to this new form of exercise, eventually she grew tired. Breathless and exhilarated, she returned to the wooden shelter and submitted to the ministrations of the dipper, who rubbed her chilled body with a towel; Agnes repaired the damage the cloth bathing cap had done to Miranda's coiffure. By the time the horse had pulled the machine out of the water and onto the shingle beach, she was dressed in her own dry clothes.

After paying the woman, she hurried home to give her aunt an enthusiastic account of the morning's activity.

"The water was not half so cold as at Scarborough, nor the breakers so strong," she said. "And I think sea-bathing is delightful!"

Long after leaving the water she continued to feel the rhythm of the waves that had caressed her. The sun and salt air had greatly improved her flagging appetite, and she looked forward to dinner for the first time in weeks. The Solway House chef, who had accompanied the family down from London, had a way with *fruits de mer* which was nothing short of masterly. The evening meal began with a delicious mullet soup, and included prawn pie, oyster patties, and lobsters taken fresh from the sea.

It was the habit of Brighton's visitors to promenade along the Steyne as the summer sun began to make its belated descent, as a prologue to the various evening entertainments. Miranda, her mood much improved, set out with her aunt and uncle at sundown.

The duchess, disappointed by the lack of persons on parade, commented that Brighton was still very thin of company and when they had taken a single turn around the grassy enclosure, she said, "I had hoped we might meet Lord Hartington. Perhaps he's at the Old Ship. Isn't there a card assembly tonight?"

"I believe so," Miranda answered absently, her attention captured by a distinguished gentleman in a dark coat. He bowed and she realised, to her dismay, that she knew him.

As he approached, her aunt asked in surprise, "Why, Mira, what is Lord Cavender doing here?"

There was no chance of avoiding an encounter; her uncle had stepped forward to shake the viscount's hand. "We are on our way to the Ship," he explained and invited his lordship to accompany them. "What brings you to Brighton, Lord Cavender? Not ill health, I hope."

"Not that, sir." When those brown eyes lingered upon her face, Miranda averted it and hoped the darkness would hide her high colour.

"I regret to say it is otherwise with me," the older man sighed. "Dr. Farquhar suggested that warm seawater baths might relieve my headaches. I've been going to William's New Baths every day, and it seems to have done some good." Glancing at his niece, he smiled and added, "Our Mira is a recent convert to bathing. She took her first plunge this morning."

The Old Ship Hotel was one of Brighton's original public houses; its assembly rooms had been added several decades earlier. The card-room was large and grand, with a vaulted ceiling adorned with plasterwork garlands and its walls decorated in the Adam style, featuring bas-relief plaques of classical figures. Mr. Forth, the master of ceremonies, led the new arrivals to a baize-covered table, and his ducal patron handed over the requisite three shillings and sixpence for refreshments. Justin tendered five shillings for himself and informed Mr. Forth of his desire to add his name to the list of subscribers.

The Duke of Solway, knowing his niece's aversion to cards, wondered if the young people might prefer to listen to the music in the adjoining room. "The duchess and I will be content playing piquet together until Mr. Forth presents another couple to make up a foursome for whist."

Although Miranda had no real desire to be alone with the viscount, she let him take her to the ballroom. Several rows of chairs, most of them occupied, were set up near the musicians' gallery for those who wished to listen to the concert in progress.

"Are you sorry that I'm here?" Justin asked over the strains of a Mozart minuet.

"Oh, no." At that moment she could not have said whether her response was the truth or merely a polite lie.

"I can't pretend that I had another purpose for coming, apart from my desire to see you."

Lacing her fingers together tightly, Miranda replied, "I should rather think you'd make an effort to avoid me."

"But then I'd have no opportunity to prove how greatly

you've misjudged me. Just as you would wish to be pardoned for an unintentional crime, I beg you to be indulgent towards me."

"You refine too much on what passed between us at our last meeting. I never implied that we cannot continue as friends."

"I retain a hope of becoming much more, in time," Justin announced before going to procure some liquid refreshment.

Miranda was glad of the opportunity to sort through her conflicting emotions. She was flattered to know that he'd followed her to Brighton, but now that the initial shock of finding him there had faded, she wondered if his uncle had ordered him to try his luck once more.

"I've been hunting for you," said a familiar voice, and she looked up to see Hart, her golden-haired cavalier, beaming down at her. He dropped into the chair next to hers, the one lately occupied by the viscount.

"The music is more to my taste than cards and gossip," she said.

"Music?" He glanced towards the gallery. "Can't even hear it. I called on you this morning, but Richards told me you'd gone bathing. How d'you like it?"

While they were comparing opinions on that interesting form of exercise, Lord Cavender returned with a glass of ratafia. Miranda performed the necessary introductions, and it was soon apparent that the two gentlemen had little in common. Hart, despite growing up at Devonshire House, cared nothing for politics, and his sympathies were wholly Whig. The viscount deftly guided the conversation out of murky and dangerous waters, and soon they were involved in an animated and rewarding discussion of horses and hunting, topics of mutual interest. By the time the duke and duchess came to collect Miranda, she was engaged to meet both gentlemen the following day at a race between the officers of a local militia company and those of the prince's regiment.

That night she fell asleep swiftly and effortlessly, and in her dreams she was floating on a calm, cool sea, while

Lord Cavender watched her, an expression of gentle amusement on his face.

In the morning Agnes bought her tea and drew back the curtains to reveal overcast skies, then assisted Miranda in putting on a white muslin gown embroidered all over with sprigs of ivy. When she hurried downstairs to breakfast, the duchess greeted her with a plaintive question.

"Mira, can you dissuade your uncle from going out in such bad weather? I have tried and failed miserably."

The duke lifted his grey head from the *Brighton Herald* and announced that he was tired of playing the invalid. "Moreover," he added, "I will not spoil Miranda's pleasure by withdrawing my escort at the last minute. You would not like her to go without me, and I can always take shelter in my carriage if it rains."

Miranda smiled her thanks as she took a piece of toast from the silver rack. Thinking it might reconcile her aunt to the excursion, she said, "I'm riding in Hart's curricle."

Mollified, the duchess replied, "I see that neither of you will be deterred, so I'm off to the dressmaker. That Frenchwoman in St. James Street has some new silks in, just in time for me to have some gowns made up. The assembly balls will begin in a few weeks."

"Don't forget to order something magnificent for the prince's birthday celebrations," the duke reminded her, his eyes softening as they rested on the dignified lady seated across from him.

Hart soon arrived to collect Miranda. Before going out to meet him she put on a hat of plaited straw and picked up a green silk parasol made in the Chinese style, with tiny tassels. Her friend failed to compliment her appearance but demanded that she tell him what she thought of his new horses.

That day set the tone for many more similar ones, and for the first time since she'd arrived in Brighton, Miranda's days were full and busy. In the morning, when the weather permitted, she went bathing; afterwards she read or wrote letters until either the marquis or the viscount—or both—called upon her. She attended a cricket match at the Royal Ground with Hart and continued to go riding with him on the downs, but he soon departed Brighton to attend the wedding of a friend. Lord Cavender redoubled his efforts to keep her entertained, taking her to a military review one day and a lecture at the Castle Inn assembly rooms the next.

"I don't think young Hartington would have appreciated the learned gentleman's discourse," Justin commented when he escorted her back to the Royal Crescent. "Even if he could have heard it."

Miranda said repressively that Hart couldn't help his infirmity. "Don't you like him? Everyone does. He is very popular."

"I confess, he has grown more popular with me since his departure."

Justin called one day while Miranda was writing a letter to her brother, and as she folded the sheet around a guinea he commented, "What a good sister you are. I hope Lord Swanborough is conscious of it."

With a rueful smile she replied, "I must plead guilty to the charge of spoiling him. Although Ninian is a full ten years my junior, we're very close, and he minds me better than he does most people."

"I shall never cease to regret that Ramsey and I grew so much apart." His expression was grave, as it always was when he mentioned his brother. "He loved sport, I devoted myself to study. I looked up to him and adored him, but he only tolerated me. After the investigation into Nick's duel he cut himself off from me—he couldn't bear my knowing the truth of how he had maligned our cousin. I hate that he was so alone when he died, but he persuaded me to leave the country. That was what he wanted."

"I never knew him very well," said Miranda, twirling her pen between her fingers. "I was only seventeen and more interested in hunters and hounds than suitors."

"And now?" he enquired.

She deemed it safer to ignore his question. "I've missed Ninian since he's been at Harrow, but he'll be coming to Brighton sometime before his next term. Uncle William and Aunt Elizabeth are the only parents he has known. Papa died the year after he was born, and our mother was never able to look after him."

"Do you remember her?" Justin prompted gently.

"How could I forget? She was so beautiful . . . and so very sad. I tried so hard to behave well when I was a child because I wanted more than anything to make her happy. She once said that if she could give me a little brother she would never cry again. And then Ninian was born, and nothing was ever the same." She inscribed Lord Swanborough's direction on the folded letter, saying matter-of-factly, "This wants a frank. I wonder whether my uncle has returned from his walk. I daresay Richards will know."

"Let me frank it for you."

He slipped the quill from her slack fingers and plunged the point into the inkwell, bending down to scrawl his name. Miranda found his proximity unsettling. His profile was strong, marked by high cheekbones and a lean, well-defined jaw, and as she stared up at his face, a wave of longing crashed over her. Bounding up from her chair, she crossed to the window in an attempt to escape the intensity of her feelings.

The day was dismal and grey; the murky sky cast its gloom over the churning sea. "It's raining," she announced. "I shall have to put off returning my books to Donaldson's."

He offered to take them for her, and overrode her objections by saying, "It's no trouble at all. I pass the library on my way back to the Castle Inn."

She went to the next room to fetch the volumes. When she gave them to him their hands brushed, and the brief contact made her heart race. It continued doing so for some time after he was gone.

She had learned a great deal that afternoon, and the fact that she loved him beyond all reason was only a part of it. Hearing him describe his feelings for Ramsey, she had realised that his brother's disgrace had affected him profoundly, the same way she was affected by her mother's madness. And like her, he kept his pain locked inside him.

Three years ago her brilliant future as a fashionable beauty had been shattered in her first season, by a woman she no longer knew, whose wild behaviour had resulted in alarming rumours. No one had ever told Miranda exactly what had transpired in that shop in Bath, and she had not wanted to ask. She knew only that the whole world, after courting her and petting her, suddenly looked askance at her for being the daughter of Lady Swanborough.

Her subsequent conversations with Lord Cavender were less serious, and several weeks passed swiftly and agreeably. The Prince of Wales arrived and opened up his pleasure palace, signalling the start of the high Season, and a host of fashionable persons descended upon Brighton in his wake. There was not a single lodging to be had; the beach was nearly obscured by bathing-machines; the circulating libraries were full of browsers and loungers, and the earlier calm of the seaside town was broken.

One night early in August a ship docked in Brighton, bringing news of a great battle in Spain. A messenger carried the despatches to His Royal Highness as he sat down to dinner, and before long the public heard that Sir Arthur Wellesley had achieved a great victory at Talavera. But the rout of the French had been costly: upwards of two thousand British soldiers had perished in the fighting.

In the Duke of Solway's household, joy was tempered with concern for Lord Edgar Marchant, an officer on Sir Arthur's staff. The duke, desperate for information about his younger son, haunted the Pavilion. Anxiety brought on the recurrence of his headaches, and while confined to his bed he studied the casualty lists printed in the newssheets. One morning the Duke of Clarence called in the Royal Crescent to tell the family that Lord Edgar had come through the battle unscathed; his name had appeared in one of Sir Arthur's dispatches.

On the twelfth of the month the bells tolled in honour of the prince's birthday, and that evening lords, ladies, the royal dukes, and other notable persons gathered at the Castle Inn for a splendid ball. The company was as brilliant as Miranda had ever seen in Brighton, and the double-cubed ballroom was uncomfortably crowded. When the Prince of Wales made his appearance, she had the dubious privilege of attracting his notice. He told her she looked like a daffodil in her yellow gown and admired her topaz necklace before retiring to the cardroom with a plump matron on his arm. He was trailed by a stout gentleman in a plain suit and a scarlet waistcoat; Lord Cavender told Miranda it was John Townsend, the famous Bow Street Runner, who served as His Royal Highness's personal bodyguard when in Brighton.

The Duchess of Solway, gowned in lavender silk and wearing a pair of amethyst ear-drops, was the most distinguished lady present. She was inclined to look down her nose at the preponderance of flushed, overdressed females bobbing about the room with their partners. Miranda carried a fan and plied it continuously but with little effect. The room was stifling, and a glass of champagne had made her feel warm.

She knew Lord Cavender had noticed her discomfort when he turned to her aunt and said, "The illuminations will begin shortly, and with Your Grace's permission I would like to take Lady Miranda outside to secure a good place."

The duchess nodded, saying, "By all means. The Duke and I will join you in a few minutes."

The couple escaped the ballroom through a side door which let onto the Pavilion grounds. A few persons stood on the lawn of the white palace, which seemed to glow in the brilliant moonlight. The cool, dew-scented air soon restored Miranda, and she laughed at her companion's criticisms of the large, glass-roofed rotunda which housed the prince's horses. Indian in design, it was heavily embellished with crenelations, arched windows, and minarets.

"This monstrosity wasn't here when I last visited Brighton," he said. "I haven't seen anything so exotic since I left Russia."

"You would do better to admire it," Miranda said. "For it cost the prince—or rather, the nation—all of seventy thousand pounds. The amount was judged excessive for a horse barn, even such an elegant one."

He suggested that they stroll through the grove which stood beside the royal stables, and as they walked along the path, arm in arm, he asked, "Have I ever told you how the Russians greet one another?"

"I don't recall that you did."

"Better still, I shall show you. But you must follow my instructions."

Intrigued, she agreed to do so.

"In Russia, whenever a lady meets a gentleman, she presents her hand—yes, like that. As the man raises it to his lips," he continued, illustrating, "she leans forward to kiss him on the forehead."

When he would not release her, she gave up the attempt to extricate herself and said softly, "Lord Cavender, you are a shameless rogue."

"You agreed to cooperate," he reminded her.

Wondering at her boldness, she bent from the waist and placed her lips lightly and tentatively upon his brow. "Is that all?" she asked warily.

He gazed down at her with eyes as dark as night. "There is a rather more universal custom which I would be happy to demonstrate."

Taking her in his arms, he pressed his mouth to hers. Although Miranda felt she ought to make some show of reluctance, however token, she discovered that she was incapable of action, caught up in the same helpless exhilaration she knew from being buffeted by the breakers. And even after he stopped kissing her, she clung to him, her cheek pressed against his until a sudden explosion made them jump.

"The fireworks have begun," said Justin as the next set of rockets went hissing towards the heavens. An instant later a spray of light flashed across the black sky.

They emerged from the grove to find a crowd massed upon the lawn, clapping and cheering with each burst of fire. A military band played, and several couples started dancing in a most abandoned fashion. No sooner had Justin restored Miranda to her relatives than the duchess decided that it was time to send for the carriage.

When Miranda gave the viscount her hand in farewell he clasped it tightly, as if to communicate something he could not say, and declared his intention of calling upon her the next day, without fail. During the short drive home she tried to interpret what had happened in the grove and found herself at a complete loss. He had not apologised, but neither had she given him cause to believe she had been insulted.

Never doubting that he would propose again, she tossed and turned for most of the night, asking herself questions which had no answers.

She realised she had been unfair to judge him so harshly for seeking a marriage of convenience, when all along her ambition had been the same. Her goal was, and had ever been, to find a husband. She loved him, and by marrying him, she could rescue him from his financial difficulties and help to placate his uncle, thereby earning his gratitude. But what if their marriage turned out as badly as that of her parents? The Earl of Swanborough had wed Lady Hermia Marchant because she had a large dowry and a duke for a brother, and even though she had borne him the much-needed heir, he must have regretted his choice.

As drowsiness overtook her at last, she wondered whether his fevered kisses meant that he cared for her. Or had his lovemaking been a clever and calculated attempt to seduce her into accepting him?

=7=

AFTER A FEW HOURS of fitful sleep, Miranda was wakened by the boom of a cannon and loud shouts. She hurried to her window and flung the curtains aside. What appeared to be half of Brighton had gathered on the beach to watch a mock battle between a fleet of yachts, one bearing the royal standard—evidently a part of the on-going festivities in honour of His Highness's birthday. Her washing water was waiting, and after her morning ablutions she took a fresh shift from her chest of drawers and covered herself with it. She put on her stockings, and when her fingers shook over the tying of her garters she tried to convince herself that it was the persistent cannon-fire which had frayed her nerves, rather than her anticipation of what the day might bring.

"The windows are rattling fit to fall out of their frames," grumbled Agnes when she brought Miranda's tea tray. "His Grace will be wanting cotton wool to put in his ears, lest all the noise bring on his headache. Now, then, what does my lady have a mind to wear? Both the blue cambric and the fawn muslin are clean and pressed."

Miranda stated her preference for the muslin. "Has my aunt risen yet?" she asked when she sat down to have her hair brushed.

"She has, and left a quarter of an hour ago for the royal chapel, thinking you wouldn't want to be disturbed."

Miranda made a haphazard selection from the tray of rings on her dressing table. Sunday, she thought thankfully, and she had no engagements; she could remain at home, waiting for Lord Cavender to call.

Shortly before noon she saw him walking along the curved pavement of the Crescent. A moment after Richards informed her of his arrival, he entered the parlour. Her panic rose, but she managed to bid him a civil, if subdued, good morning.

"You know why I've come."

She had neither the energy nor the wit to deny it. The sofa had sufficient room for two persons, but she did not think she could walk that far on her watery legs, and sank down abruptly onto an armless chair.

"I could not speak last night," he said, following her. "I wanted to give you time to reflect and consider. I came to Brighton hoping to repair the false impression you had when I last begged the honour of making you my wife. If you still doubt my purpose, let me assure you that it was not your portion which my uncle cared about so much as the simple fact that he was once fond of your mother."

"He knew her?"

"Years ago, before his family packed him off to India. He told me you'd gone to London with the intent of finding a husband, and that is why I was emboldened to speak to you as precipitately as I did." Justin took up a position behind her chair and placed one hand on her shoulder. "If Damon hadn't told you about Uncle Isaac's plan that we should marry, which I alone had the right to disclose, would you have accepted me?"

"I—I suppose so," she admitted, thankful that he couldn't see her face.

"I won't deny that our marriage has been arranged, after a fashion," she heard him say, "but that doesn't mean we can't be happy together. You won't be wed to a nobody . . . between them, Lord Granville and Mr. Canning will find a place for me at the Foreign Office. And as Lady Cavender, you will be mistress of a handsome property."

"I am fully conscious of the advantages of becoming your wife, Lord Cavender."

When he placed his hand beneath her elbow, forcing her to rise and face him, she saw that he wore a grave expression. "Miranda, I value your candour, so if you have any lingering concerns, you must tell me."

Unable to resist the appeal in his brown eyes, she said, "My only reservation is on your lordship's account. You know of my mother's condition, and I fear that I might pass her sickness to my own children, who would be your heirs. The possibility must worry you."

"Yes." The simple word was like a blow, but his next words softened it. "I do worry because I see how much it alarms you. It needn't, Miranda. It mustn't." Taking her hand, Justin gave her a sunny smile. "You ought to know, if you don't already, that a propensity for drink and gaming runs in the Blythe family. Happily, I have been spared, but if our sons should turn out drunkards and wastrels, I want you to know where to lay the blame."

He must be desperate to free himself from those mortgages, she thought as he pulled her close, holding her against his heart as he had done in the pavilion grove. "Say yes," he pleaded, before tilting her chin up so she could receive his kiss.

They were too much concerned with the business at hand to hear the door open, or to notice that the Duke of Solway stood upon the threshold, an interested observer to their impassioned embrace. After a moment he rapped softly upon the doorsill, and the startled couple broke apart. "Miranda," he said with unimpaired calm, "I thought you might like to walk along the downs, but I see you've found your own entertainment."

Making a hasty adjustment to his cravat, Justin announced, "Sir, your niece has honoured me by accepting my offer of marriage."

"Has she indeed?" Advancing into the room, he shook Justin's hand. "I wish you both very happy, and I'm sure the duchess will add her felicitations to mine."

Justin said wryly, "It was my impression that she was looking rather higher than a viscount in straitened circumstances." When he saw his betrothed's troubled frown, he told her, "It's no more than the truth, however much I regret it."

"My wife and I have always agreed that our ward should follow her own inclinations," the duke replied. He pressed Miranda's hand before ceremoniously presenting it to Justin. "I shall not impose upon you any longer, for I'm sure you have much to discuss."

No sooner had he left the couple alone than they found themselves completely tongue-tied. After a brief and mortified silence, Miranda was sufficiently mistress of herself to say, "I never quite said yes."

"Oh, but you did," he maintained.

She gave a self-conscious laugh, then asked him when he wished to be married.

"Whenever they let us," he answered. "Your uncle's lawyers and mine must meet and draw up the necessary contracts, and I expect that will take some considerable time, my affairs being in such disarray. And although my tenant has stated he will vacate Cavender Chase at Michaelmas, until it is made ready, I've no place to keep you." Justin ran his fingers through his hair, saying, "I shall give you a ring to seal our pledge, of course. The Blythe emeralds were sold long ago, to pay off my father's creditors, but perhaps it's just as well, for sapphires are a better compliment to your eyes."

As he led her over to the sofa, she warned herself not to put too much faith in such lover-like remarks, for this match was being made for their mutual convenience and she would do well to remember it. For all his endearing honesty, he still had not admitted that Mr. Meriden was going to forgive his debt on their wedding day. But it was not unreasonable to hope that in time his feelings for her might grow into something stronger than friendly affection, more lasting than gratitude.

The forthcoming marriage would not be made public until the principals returned to town, but Justin suspected that the gossips of Brighton had already communicated the state of affairs to all parts of the nation. He had seen to it that Lady Miranda's slim white hand was suitably adorned with a fine sapphire surrounded by starry diamonds, and the couple were often absent from the local assemblies, preferring to pursue their better acquaintance in private. To his great relief, the duchess, who had received the news of the betrothal with complaisance, treated him as one of the family, inviting him to dine in the Royal Crescent as often as he pleased.

When the duke expressed the hope that his niece would want to be married in the chapel at Haberdine Castle, Justin, knowing Miranda regarded it as her home, assented. He also endorsed her wish for a quiet wedding. But the October date he put forward was deemed unacceptable by the Marchants; their participation in the Jubilee celebrations would keep them tied to London. And because Granville had written to say there might be a great shakeup in the Foreign Office before long, Justin was reluctant to make any firm plans for November or December, and Parliament would convene in January. He thought he might be able to set aside a few days at the end of the year for the business of being married, and when Miranda told him her family would be in residence at Haberdine during Christmas, he suggested New Year's Eve as an appropriate date for their nuptials. The choice won the unanimous approval of all parties concerned.

As August gave way to September, Justin was preoccupied with the pleasant duty of dancing attendance upon his hard-won lady, and his appreciation of her increased with each passing day. From their first meeting he had been conscious of her beauty; her graceful manners and lively wit had long enchanted him. She had grown up under the influence of a staunch supporter of the Government party and therefore possessed an acute understanding of the political situation. There was no need to explain the ramifications of the Duke of Portland's illness; she knew it perfectly well, and unlike Justin, was actually acquainted with the prime minister. Because she had a cousin serving in the Peninsula, she was interested in current military operations and had read the accounts of Lord Chatham's failed mission and the reports of the fever epidemic which was raging through the army encamped at Walcheren. She had long acted as an unofficial secretary to her guardian and proved willing, even eager, to do the same for Justin, who formed the habit of composing his letters to Lord Granville in the sunny front parlour of the house in the Royal Crescent. She mended his quills better than he could himself and used his weak eyesight as an excuse for reading to him from the papers.

"Don't imagine I'm making a martyr of myself," she replied when he asked if she was not bored. "I act from pure self-interest, for I aspire to create a political salon for our party as Lady Holland and Lady Bessborough have done for the Whigs."

Had he not been a little bit in love, he wouldn't have offered for her; that he would swiftly become enraptured was a complete revelation to him. Her encouraging reception of his ever-increasing ardour delighted him, and as the early weeks of their engagement passed, he became intimately acquainted with the satin texture of her ebony hair and the rose-petal softness of her skin. He was already familiar with her soft and pliant lips. Sometimes he wondered which of her former suitors had tutored her so well, and whenever his cousin's name obtruded into these ruminations, he banished it quickly.

September was little more than a week old when he received a letter from Lord Granville which caused him to revise his opinion that he was quite the luckiest fellow in the world. Reluctant though he was to deliver desperate tidings at an early hour, he set forth on his ritual morning promenade from the Castle Inn to the duke's house. He found Miranda alone, her head bent over a volume of fashion plates.

At his entrance she cast it aside and rose from the sofa, saying, "You very nearly missed me. I was on the point of leaving for my morning plunge."

"I won't detain you for very long." Reaching into his

coat pocket, he withdrew his friend's missive. "According to Granville, Canning has resigned as foreign secretary."

"Has he? And yet," she said as she unfolded the letter, "it is not such a surprise."

"I'd hoped it might be averted," he sighed. "Granville reveals only the facts of Canning's decision, not the reason for it."

"There can only be one—Castlereagh's mismanagement of our military operations in Spain and Portugal. And now the failure of the Walcheren expedition has added to Mr. Canning's grievances."

"I heard a rumour some months ago that he was trying to persuade Portland to organise the War Office along different lines. He could not be content so long as Castlereagh remained in a position of power," Justin said.

"But with the Duke of Portland so unwell and likely to step down, didn't Mr. Canning have hopes of becoming prime minister himself?"

"I don't know." Justin shrugged. "He was never a favourite with the king, partly because of his support of Catholic emancipation. By relinquishing his seat in the Cabinet, he seems to have scuttled what might have been a brilliant future."

"And scuttled your future as well," she said sympathetically.

Justin sat down beside her on the sofa. "Don't repine on my account. Canning is more an acquaintance than a friend, and I still have Granville as an ally."

When he fell silent, Miranda turned her attention to the letter. "He advises you to hasten to town."

"I mean to do so, little though I like it."

"But you must go." She looked as if she might have said something more but had changed her mind. Going to the writing desk, she told him the day's post had brought her two letters. "One comes from your mother, and you must advise me how to reply. She has offered to make Cavender Chase habitable for us, and though it is very kind of her, it will put her to a deal of trouble."

"She knows better than you or I how many servants

must be engaged and which rooms stand in need of refurbishment. And I would prefer that the household be running smoothly when I take you to Wiltshire this autumn."

Miranda then showed him the note of felicitation she had received from her cousin Lady Blythe, and not long after she raised a question Justin had been dreading for some time. "I've heard nothing from Damon. Have you not written him the news of our engagement?"

"No. Not yet. That is to say, I'm not perfectly sure where he may be staying, I know only that his journey took him to the Lakes." He would not reveal to her what had passed between his cousin and himself; she was clever enough to guess that she'd been the cause of their rift. Neither was he eager to inform Damon of his matrimonial plans. Let him learn of the betrothal from the society columns of the *Gazette*, along with the rest of the world, he thought with unwonted venom.

"I wonder where he can be," Miranda said, perplexed. "Surely he hasn't been in Cumberland this long while. I think he must have returned to town by now, don't you, my lord?"

Provoked by her abiding interest in his cousin's whereabouts, Justin answered sharply, "Must you persist with this needless formality? I should think by now you'd be able to address me by my given name. I have no wish to continue as 'my lord' when one of my own relations is 'Damon' to you."

Her manner was decidedly cool when she replied, "You ought to have made your wishes plainer."

His outburst, rather than promoting intimacy, had resulted in constraint and he regretted it. For the remainder of his visit, she maintained so rigid a reserve that he longed to shake her, or kiss her. Or both. To avoid making matters worse, he did neither.

"I have much to do before my departure," he said, climbing to his feet, "and I'm keeping you from your morning dip. Go turn yourself into a nymph of the sea. I shall return later in the day."

The London mail departed Brighton at seven o'clock

each evening. The coach was often full, and when Justin stopped at the post office to book a seat he was surprised to find one still available. He spent the day packing and paying farewell calls on those of his friends who would be offended if he failed to take his leave of them. After his trunks were corded and carried out of his rooms, he returned to the Royal Crescent to bid the Marchants—and Miranda—farewell.

The prospect of separation was a bleak one. When the duke and duchess discreetly followed the tea tray out of the room, Justin silently blessed them, and he joined Miranda on the window-seat, determined to make things right with her. "I hope my behaviour this morning hasn't dissuaded you from having me as your husband," he said, smiling, and to his great relief, she laughed.

"I've no wish to play the jilt, and with the news about Canning you've already suffered enough disappointment today." Pillowing her head against his shoulder, Miranda added, "It's curious, but I feel better now we've had our first quarrel."

"And our first chance to kiss and make up." He touched his lips to her brow, then her nose, and finally brought them to rest upon her rosy mouth.

Justin reached town just after the resignation of the prime minister, the ailing Duke of Portland, was announced. Lord Castlereagh of the War Office also resigned, having learned of Mr. Canning's secret plot to force him from his post. For the next week the city seethed with talk of the political calamity; by night it was plagued by riot. The people of London refused to pay the higher prices Mr. Kemble had instigated at his new Covent Garden Theatre and resorted to violence when he failed to return to the old system of pricing.

The servants at Elston House had no news of their master and knew not when his lordship would return. After Justin had reclaimed his former quarters, he left Berkeley Square for Lord Granville's house but found that his friend had gone out. When he chanced to meet

Lady Bessborough's carriage in Piccadilly, he sought information about Granville, but curiously she was more eager to relate the current *on-dit*.

"Have you heard the latest about poor Lord Chatham?" she asked, referring to the leader of the ill-fated Walcheren expedition. "They're saying he'll be created the Marquis of Walcher-*out*."

Justin's laughter was merely a polite response, for Chatham's failure to destroy the French ships in the Scheldt was far from amusing. In his opinion, Mr. Canning's complaints about Lord Castlereagh's management of the War Office were not entirely without foundation. "Have you seen Granville?" he asked her. "I left Brighton at his request, but when I called in Stanhope Street he was not at home."

Her ladyship's merry smile vanished in an instant. "Perhaps he had to attend a meeting of the Cabinet. His lordship has only just returned from a visit to the Beauforts. Did you know he chased Harriet Cavendish to Badminton House? He had hopes of persuading her to marry him, but nothing came of it."

Her perturbation was evident to Justin, who sincerely pitied her. He knew of her long *affaire* with his friend, for Granville once admitted that Lady Bessborough had borne him two children.

On Wednesday of that week Justin called at Gloucester Lodge near Brompton, where he found Mr. Canning in a more sanguine mood than his situation seemed to warrant. He professed to have thrown his support to Spencer Perceval, the gentleman most likely to succeed the Duke of Portland as prime minister. Mr. Joseph Planta, a secretary at the Foreign Office, was the only other visitor that day, and the three gentlemen were imbibing port and talking of Russian affairs when a footman entered with a letter for Mr. Canning.

"From Castlereagh," he reported as he broke the seal. "Three full sheets." For a moment he reviewed them silently, then exclaimed, "By God, I had rather fight than read the whole!"

"Is it a challenge?" asked Mr. Planta, jumping to his feet as if eager to avenge his former superior.

"Precisely that," Mr. Canning replied grimly. "He concludes, 'Under the circumstances I must require that satisfaction from you to which I feel myself entitled to lay claim. I have the honour to be, sir, your humble obedient servant, Castlereagh.' " Turning upon Justin, he said, "Cavender, I'm glad you're here—I need a messenger." He sat down at once to pen his reply, saying regretfully that he had no choice but to accept the challenge. "I'll not be branded a coward by refusing him the satisfaction he demands. Lord Cavender, pray deliver this into Castlereagh's hand and inform him that my second will call upon his to arrange a meeting."

Justin, who had once served his cousin Dominic in that capacity, offered his services. Mr. Canning bestowed a grateful smile upon him but said, "I cannot let you become embroiled in this affair, my lord, lest it impair your chances of preferment. I had better rely upon one of my intimates. I expect Charles Ellis will oblige me."

"Sir," Mr. Planta interjected, "he is at Claremont, in attendance upon Her Majesty."

"Henry Wellesley, then—it makes no odds. I prefer Wellesley, he needs something to distract him from this plaguey divorce. Will you call upon him, Cavender, and ask if he will come to me?"

Justin journeyed back to London posthaste, consoling himself for being left out of the momentous undertaking with the reminder that at least he would be spared the harm of any resultant scandal.

Mr. Henry Wellesley, brother of the newly made Lord Wellington of Talavera, would not assist Mr. Canning for fear of endangering the pending divorce action against his wife, who had eloped with Lord Paget in the spring. "But I can go to Claremont and rescue Charles Ellis from the queen, and then he'll be free to do whatever Canning requires. It may be," he added hopefully, "that he will manage to smooth things over with Castlereagh."

But the next morning Justin received a brief note from

Mr. Canning which proved that Mr. Ellis's attempt to mediate had failed. "My Lord Cavender," it read, "Castlereagh and I met at Putney Heath at sunrise. In the second exchange of fire I received a wound in the thigh but am in no danger. I stand very much in your lordship's debt—G.C."

For the rest of the day Justin remained at Elston House, beginning but never completing a letter to Miranda. His only visitor was an outraged Lord Granville, who announced his decision to resign as war secretary. He would not, he said furiously, continue to work with Castlereagh, who had so slighted the honour of his friend Canning. Justin knew better than to try and change his mind, but his spirits sank.

When he was alone again, Justin balled up the unfinished letter and cast it into the fire. His surviving hope for a government post had lain with Granville; he was not well enough acquainted with Mr. Perceval to depend on his aid. How, he wondered despondently, would Miranda react to everything that happened? Poor girl, her political salon was no more than an air-dream now, as she would learn when she read tomorrow's *Gazette*. He had no way to prepare her for the disappointment in store.

Justin was roused from his mournful reverie by the pound of the door-knocker. "What now?" he muttered, climbing to his feet reluctantly.

To his great astonishment, a woman was shown in. He stared at her wordlessly, too bemused to voice the warm welcome she evidently expected, for she hurried across the room, hands outstretched. He took them in his own and lifted her fingers to his lips as she leaned forward to kiss his brow, in the Russian fashion.

"My dear Natasha, this is a surprise," he told her, keeping to himself the fact that it was not necessarily a welcome one.

"I wanted to bring the children, but I left them at the hotel with my maid, a stupid *françoise*. Feo wants to see you, but he was sick on the journey and has not quite recovered. My Ivanushka is, as you English say, perfectly stout."

"How long have you been in London?"

"Two days only," she replied, untying the strings of her bonnet. "And such a difficulty I had finding you! So many nobles live here. I asked *le concierge* where was Cavender House, and he said it belonged to a lord named Blythe."

"My cousin Dominic," Justin explained. "My father sold it years ago."

"To me it has been a riddle, for when I demanded to know where I would find Lord Cavender, I was told to try *Elston* House."

"I'm staying with my other cousin, the marquis," Justin explained. "I have no town residence of my own."

"Nor I," she said, dimpling at him. "Not yet, though I must begin looking. Your London is so large, but already I know the best streets. And the shops! *Mon dieu*, the English ladies are fortunate!"

Justin rang for refreshment, and when it was brought the princess admired the Staffordshire cups and saucers and commended the excellence of the teacakes. She described her journey and vented her frustration at finding her relatives out of town. And when she seemed to expect that Justin would escort her to Wilton House to visit her cousin, he knew it was time to broach the difficult subject of his engagement.

"Natasha," he said gently, when she seemed to have run out of breath, "I'm afraid I cannot leave town just now. People would think it odd. You see, I'm going to be married."

"Married!" she gasped.

"Last month I became engaged to Lady Miranda Peverel. Her uncle is a duke, a very influential man. We will be wed at the end of the year."

"Have you known her a long time?"

"I met her the day I returned to London."

Her hazel eyes registered pain but her voice was steady when she asked, "Shall you present me to her?"

"I will be happy to do so, but just now she's staying at a place called Brighton, which is by the sea. Many English go there for amusement, or to improve their health."

"Your lady is an *invalide*?" He answered her with a shake of his head. Reaching for her sable muff, Natasha said hastily, "I must not stay; I only wished to pay my respects. Will I see you again soon, *mon cher*?"

"I shall call upon you tomorrow, to see how Prince Feodor improves. Perhaps we might go walking in the park. Have you seen it yet, or only the shops?" he quizzed her.

He went with her to her carriage and opened the door himself, but before she let him hand her in she said softly, "You are a man of your word, dear friend, for when we parted you told me if I came to England I would find you still a single man. You only failed to warn me that you might be promised to another."

Her laugh seemed forced and did not ease Justin's mind of the suspicion that she felt slighted by his betrothal.

=8=

THE TROUBLESOME MONTH of September was nearing its end when the Marchants and their niece returned to London. Justin called at Solway House the day after they arrived and was told by Richards that he would find the young ladyship in the gardens. Making his way to the rear of the house, he walked through the flower-scented conservatory and exited through the glass doors opening onto the terrace. Of Miranda he saw no sign, but a dark-haired boy stood before the marble fountain, prodding a miniature sailboat with a long stick.

Looking up, he surveyed Justin calmly, and with no evidence of shyness announced, "I'm Swanborough."

Justin, gazing down at another version of the face he had been missing, answered, "And I'm Cavender, the fellow who's going to marry your sister."

"I thought you must be." Ninian Peverel poked his boat with the stick, guiding it away from the cascade of water. His glossy black curls were cut in a cherubim style, the only thing about him which was angelic. He had a pointed chin with a decided cleft, and his eyes, so darkly blue that they seemed black, contained a spark of devilment. "Mira went inside," he announced. "She had a letter from Damon and was laughing so hard she began to cry. Damon fell off a donkey."

"Good," Justin muttered before he could stop himself.

"Don't you like him?"

"I love him as a brother," he pronounced with a virtuous

97

air. A conniving and treacherous brother, he added silently.

Ninian, righting his craft, said, "Next week I return to Harrow. Where did you go to school?"

"I'm an Etonian," Justin answered, hoping this would not discredit him in those shrewd, critical eyes.

"The masters at Eton are said to be even worse than ours." Ninian's dark brows drew together. "I didn't want to leave Brighton. I went in the sea—I can swim like a duck—and Uncle William said I might go out on a boat if I wished. But it rained a great deal and then we came to London, which I loathe."

Not knowing what was required of him, Justin said he was sorry to hear it.

"Shall I go and find my sister?"

"I would be very much obliged if you would."

"Here," the boy said, thrusting the stick into Justin's hand. "Mind *Victorious* for me."

It was not long before Miranda emerged from the conservatory, looking many times lovelier than when Justin had left her in Brighton. She greeted him with evident pleasure. "So you've met Ninian," she said, sitting upon the edge of the fountain.

"Yes, he was telling me how much he regretted leaving the seaside."

"He hates London," she said, shaking her head. "And he makes faces at the second footman, whom he has taken into dislike. At breakfast he told Aunt Elizabeth that she had better get rid of the cook—last night his hot milk had skin on it. If it happens again, he intends to run away. He probably would, too—he's such an odd boy."

"And very like you in looks, if not in disposition. Had you an easy journey from Brighton?"

"We reached London in good time, yes." She plunged her fingers into the water and made waves that rocked the tiny boat. "I've just had a letter from Damon."

"So I heard," said Justin, keeping his eye on the vessel under his command.

"Yours to him must have gone astray—he read about the betrothal in the newspaper!"

"Did he?" Justin dared not admit to her that no letter had been posted.

"He has been paying country visits, and his travels have taken him to Badminton and Chatsworth. Trust Damon to find a more comfortable billet than a waterside inn! I think his patience ran out when his friends induced him to go riding 'round one of the lakes on a donkey. He took a tumble. Damon, who so prides himself on his horsemanship!" Laughing, she dried her fingers with a lace-edged handkerchief. "I wish I might have seen it!"

"And I," Justin said feelingly.

"He'll be in town for the Jubilee. I quite long to see him again, don't you?" She looked up at him in the expectation that he would agree and he nodded. "You must have been very busy lately—I've not had a letter for ages."

He said heavily, "The government is in disarray, ministers are quarrelling and resigning in droves, and a large part of our army has succumbed to yellow fever."

"I know it. I wasn't scolding you."

"I do have some happy news," he told her on a brighter note. "The Shah of Persia is so disturbed by Napoleon's failure to live up to the Treaty of Finkenstein that he's making overtures again, and last spring Harford Jones persuaded him to sign a preliminary treaty of friendship and alliance. Now we're drawing up a more substantive pact, and a Persian envoy will arrive here soon. Granville suggested to Mr. Perceval that I should be employed in the negotiations. He was kind enough to say I showed some aptitude for it during his second mission to Russia."

"Oh, Justin, I am glad." Miranda reached out to touch his sleeve.

"I'm hopeful that this business with Persia can be concluded to our advantage, for she will be an important and necessary ally. The shah has already repudiated his former treaty with France, which might have given Napoleon a dangerous right of passage to India and our territories there. The effect upon trade would have been even more ruinous than the present blockades." Capturing her hand, he said playfully, "If I succeed in my endeavour, I might become ambassador to Persia. Could you support living in a tent on the desert, surrounded by camels?"

"Perfectly well, for I've heard that Eastern princes are divinely handsome."

He tightened his clasp. "And one of them will try to steal you from me and shut you up in his *andarun*—that's what the Persians call their harem." She blushed, betraying her consciousness of what such a life entailed, and he laughed. "Well, very soon I shall be able to shut you away in my own palace. Which reminds me, my mother wants to know when we will join her at Cavender Chase. Tell me how soon I may carry you off to Wiltshire."

"Here comes my aunt. You must ask her."

The duchess and young Lord Swanborough joined them, and when Justin put his question to her she replied, "Mira and I should be able to leave London within a fortnight. If we begin ordering her bride-clothes immediately, they can be fitted upon our return and finished before we leave for Haberdine. And the duke is determined that Lawrence should paint her, although one hundred guineas for a portrait seems excessive to me. But Hoppner, who painted her mother, is too ill to undertake the commission."

Justin, knowing how little Miranda wanted to be reminded of Lady Swanborough, made haste to change the subject, and began talking of the theatre riots. "The new Covent Garden is quite splendid, but I fear the mob will pull it down if Kemble doesn't agree to go back to the old prices."

"*I* want to go to Sadler's Wells to see an aquatic spectacle," young Ninian said in his determined way.

"You, my fine gentleman, are in disgrace," his aunt replied tartly. "And unless we see a marked improvement in your manners, you'll have no such treat."

When Lord Swanborough scowled, his soft-hearted sister turned an imploring face to Justin and said she was sure Lord Cavender had found nothing amiss with

Ninian's behaviour. Justin, after supporting this assertion, offered to take Ninian to the Wells himself, and the duchess agreed to let him go, albeit reluctantly.

During the days before the young earl was dispatched to Harrow, he and his future brother-in-law became firm friends. One afternoon when Justin escorted Miranda home from Mr. Lawrence's house in Russell Square, she expressed her relief that he and Ninian were on such good terms.

"With him there is no middle ground," she explained. "He either loves people or despises them."

"What do you hear from him since his incarceration?"

"Well, he hasn't been thrashed yet. Aunt Elizabeth and I plan to visit him on Sunday."

"Might I go with you? I see you so rarely these days, and all your dressmakers and milliners and painters seem not to care that I might have some claim upon your time."

This speech delighted Miranda, although she took care not to show it. "Soon we'll depart for Cavender Chase, where you'll have a surfeit of my company."

"Impossible," he declared.

On Sunday afternoon they set out for Harrow-on-the-Hill in one of the duke's comfortable travelling carriages, and the weather was so fine that the ladies lowered the windows to let in the cool, fresh air. Miranda caught sight of the the tall spire of Saint Mary's just as the coachman began to slow the pace as they ascended the rise of ground on which sat church, village, and school.

She leaned out of the open window to wave at her brother, who stood at the door of his boarding house. "There's someone with him," she announced when she saw Ninian's companion.

This individual, a solemn boy with soulful eyes, was a stranger to her but not to Justin, whom he greeted with grave formality. "*Monsieur*, I am very glad to see you," he said when Lord Cavender emerged from the carriage. "Is *Maman* well? Does she send a message for me?"

"Alas, I have no tidings of your mother," Justin replied,

"for she has been staying at a place called Wilton. Your Grace, I present to you Prince Feodor Levaskov, my friend from Russia and my former pupil. Feodor Pavlovich, this is the Duchess of Solway, and Lord Swanborough's sister, Lady Miranda Peverel."

The young prince bowed to both ladies. Ninian, who did not stand upon form, demanded that they dine at the Crown and Anchor, as Feodor was new to Harrow and had not been there.

"Very well," the duchess said calmly, "let us go at once. I'm quite sure you are about to tell me you're both starving." During the short walk to the village she catechised her nephew, trying to determine how diligent he was in his studies.

By the time they arrived at the inn, Miranda had learned that her brother's comrade was the elder son of Princess Natalia Levaskov, a name already familiar to her from Justin's reminiscences of Russia. She inferred from the child's discourse that Justin had been a regular caller during the Levaskovs' stay at Nerot's Hotel and wondered that he should have neglected to inform her of the princess's visit to England.

"Do you know if *Maman* has found herself a house?" Feodor asked Justin.

"She has, in Brook Street, and I believe she and Ivanushka will remove to it as soon as she returns to town. How do you like it here? Are they treating you well?"

"Yes, but the masters are strict," said Feodor. "We have games, very rough sometimes. I wish Ninian to teach me the cricket, but he prefers to row on the lake."

When they arrived at the Crown and Anchor, Justin bespoke a parlour and said he would treat the boys to whatever delicacies they desired. The ladies advised the earl and the prince not to bolt their food, but neither heeded the warning, and when the meal was over the waiter presented their host with a long bill cataloguing the many pies, pastries, and cakes the pair had consumed. By the time they were deposited on the doorstep of their boarding house, both complained of stomach-ache.

"Poor things," Miranda sighed as the carriage made the slow descent of the hill, "they will be up all night."

"I pity their housemaster's wife," her aunt commented, "for she will be the one to sit with them. I ought never to have let them eat so much."

Justin, seated with his back to the horses, leaned slightly forward and said, "I'm curious to know why Lord Swanborough, the ward of a leading Tory, is receiving his education at that bastion of Whigdom. Was his father a Harrovian?"

"Yes," Miranda told him, "but there was another reason. Eton, perhaps because it enjoys the patronage of the king, attaches more importance to rank. Uncle William hoped Harrow would cure Ninian of his tendency to rule. It hasn't, of course, and the boys in his form follow him slavishly. Prince Feodor is his latest victim, but he seems to be sensible enough not to let my brother get him into any serious trouble."

"I ought to warn Princess Levaskov that her princeling has got into bad company, but out of consideration for you I shall describe Lord Swanborough as a young man of character."

Laughing, Miranda said, "Taking care to refrain from any definition of his character—what a diplomat you are! Did I hear you say that the princess is visiting Wilton?"

"The Countess of Pembroke is her cousin. She is related to Count Simon Woronzov, who was the Russian ambassador for so many years."

When they reached Solway House, Justin accepted the ladies' invitation to come inside, not, as Miranda had supposed, because he hoped for a *tête-à-tête* with her but from a desire to speak with her aunt. She left them together in the green salon and went upstairs to pen a letter to her cousin Nerissa.

The duchess, puzzled by his lordship's request for an audience, turned questioning grey eyes upon him. "I imagine your business concerns my niece in some way."

"And Lady Swanborough," he surprised her by saying. "Has Miranda ever a desire to visit her mother?"

"Never," the duchess said emphatically. "She never speaks of Hermia, not since the incident at Bath, which you must have heard about by now. Tell me, Lord Cavender, what exactly are you suggesting?"

"Cavender Chase lies within an hour of Bath, and it occurred to me that if Miranda cared to see Lady Swanborough she might do so while we are there. I wished to bring up the possibility before we leave town, that any necessary arrangements might be made in advance."

"No arrangements are required; Hermia is able to receive visitors. The duke has seen his sister several times and was glad of it, but whether Mira would be I cannot say. She becomes agitated very easily, and we have been careful to shield her from certain unpleasant facts about her mother's condition. And although Hermia is doing very well at present, a visit from Miranda might do more harm than good."

"Lady Swanborough is in the care of a physician, is she not? He would be able to offer an opinion, and if you will be so good as to give me the direction I shall write to him by the next post." Justin put on his spectacles and took a pencil and his memorandum book from his coat pocket.

"Dr. Mostyn, Paragon Buildings." When he had made the notation, the duchess commented, "There was a time, not so long ago, when I wanted to marry Miranda to a marquis—first Elston, and more recently Lord Hartington. You had the duke's support from the beginning, and it was not my place to raise any objections to the match. But as I come to know you better, I share his belief that Mira made the best choice."

Early in October, Spencer Perceval became prime minister and before his predecessor had even surrendered his seals of office he set about forming an administration. Mr. Canning remained at Gloucester Lodge recuperating from his bullet wound, and when he heard that Perceval hoped to have the Marquis Wellesley as foreign secretary, he predicted that his lordship would refuse.

Miranda, closely following these developments, hoped otherwise. Lord Wellesley, who had been posted to Spain as ambassador in July, was one of her uncle's cronies. But she had little opportunity to discuss this development with Justin, for she saw him seldom; he was so often in Downing Street, familiarising himself with Persian affairs. Her days were busy as well, and the endless sittings and fittings were so tedious that she longed to escape with him to Wiltshire.

Once, when he escorted her to an evening party she met Lord Hartington, whose lighthearted felicitations showed that he had no regrets about her engagement. Justin's friend Lord Granville Leveson-Gower was there also, flirting with a lady Miranda had never seen before. She had a round, dimpled face and soft brown hair, and her gown of russet velvet was cut low, displaying a voluptuous bosom. A strand of opals, each as large as a shilling piece adorned her neck, which Miranda decided was a trifle short.

"Who is that with Granville?" she asked Hart curiously.

"Someone he knew in Russia. She's a princess, some cousin of Lady Pembroke's—I forget the name," he said, shrugging.

"Levaskov?"

"Yes, that's the one. I say, let's join this set . . . Cavender's a good chap, he will not mind your dancing with me."

Their reel left her breathless, for Hart had spun her about mercilessly. She had no time to recover before Justin reclaimed her and said he wanted to present her to the princess. She was happy to meet the foreign lady, although intens scrutiny from a pair of hazel eyes was disconcerting. "I'm glad to make the acquaintance of one of Lord Cavender's Russian friends," she said truthfully, "for it's not a pleasure I shall have very often."

"Not unless milord should take you in Russia," Natasha replied.

"I would like to, but with this war, it may not be possible for many years," Justin said before moving away to speak to Sir George Beaumont.

Miranda asked the princess how long she would be in England.

"When Lord Cavender lived in Russia he often said he could happily remain there always, and I feel much the same about his country. The landscape is beautiful and so very green, but the people I find odd and puzzling—reserved, and yet so very informal. And although the gentlemen are clever, the ladies seem to me quite dull. Few of the noble English girls are educated in schools such as the Smolny Institute, where I was a pupil. The only accomplishments they possess seem to me to be . . . is the word frivolous?"

Miranda nodded, for she had sometimes shared that opinion. "In our society a depth of knowledge can be a liability. It is sufficient for a young lady to play the pianoforte, sew a little, and acquire a smattering of drawing-room French."

"My cousin Catherine, Lady Pembroke, translated a French tragedy into Russian when she was but twelve—a great achievement, *non*? She tells me that instruction would be wasted on English ladies, for after they marry they cease almost to exist. The money, even of an heiress, belongs to her husband. It is barbarous!" Natasha lifted her dimpled chin and said proudly, "In Russia the wife's property and fortune remain her own, to be passed down to her heirs. When my brother married me to Prince Paul, I kept my house in Moscow and my country estates at Droskoe and in Poland. But I talk too much," she concluded, "and it is not *convenable* for me to criticise a country where I am a visitor."

"I met your son last week at Harrow," Miranda informed her. "He and my brother are schoolmates."

"Yes, of Lord Swanborough I have heard very much. My Feo's letters are so full of 'Ninian'. I will meet him soon, for Lord Cavender has promised to take me to the school before he leaves for Wiltshire."

As Justin had failed to mention this to Miranda, she found herself at a disadvantage.

"Lord Granville is naughty," Natasha observed, a laugh in her voice. "Only see how he is making up to that plain lady, and after being so devoted to me all night! These Englishmen break hearts—it is their habit—especially the hearts of Russian ladies. My friend Eudoxie, the Princess Galitzen, believed he would marry her. And I also have suffered pain because of such inconstancy," she sighed.

"Lord Granville is expected to wed Lady Harriet Cavendish," Miranda informed her, wondering why she should be the recipient of these confidences.

"A beauty would despair of holding that one. I did believe the nobles of your country were permitted to marry for love, but Lord Cavender has told me it is seldom true."

Had Justin told the Princess Levaskov that his own marriage was a loveless one? Miranda had hoped to be friends with the Russian lady but now feared it could never be. When she recalled that he'd lived in her home for more than a year, she felt that she was the outsider, not the princess.

The Duchess of Solway seldom stayed late at a party, no matter how brilliant, and it was not long before she called her niece to her side and announced her intended departure. Justin, to Miranda's considerable relief, elected to leave at the same time. As they stood in the vestibule waiting for their carriage, she confirmed her aunt's belief that the rooms had been too crowded and the musicians deplorable.

"The little Russian appears to have made a hit," the duchess declared. "Has she been widowed very long?"

Justin said in a subdued voice, "Prince Paul Levaskov died a year ago, after a long illness."

Miranda was wondering to what extent he had comforted the princess—before and after her husband's demise—when she heard her aunt say, "Most likely she has come to England to look for a husband." Assailed by a terrible suspicion, one that had been growing in her mind without her being fully aware, she looked over at Justin. Was he the cause of that heartache the princess had alluded to? Suddenly anxious to depart for Wiltshire, she comforted herself with the thought that Cavender Chase, which represented their future together, would provide her a happy escape from an unwelcome reminder of his past.

=9=

MIRANDA, WITH HER aunt and Justin, departed London early one morning, and managed to cover ninety miles to Cavender Chase in a single day. A mile or so beyond Calne they abandoned the main turnpike to Bath for a narrower, more winding road which brought them to the lodge gates. Miranda first saw the park and the palatial stone mansion in the faint light of dusk.

The viscountess greeted them in the hall, and after welcoming Miranda to the Chase, she invited the ladies to warm themselves at the marble fireplace, fully large enough for roasting an ox. "How handsome you look, Elizabeth," she greeted the duchess, "but it was ever true. Are you weary? My health is much improved from former days, but I should be thoroughly worn down by the drive from London. If you but follow Mary, she will show you up to your rooms. There is no need to rush about changing, we don't dine for another two hours."

Later the company reassembled in a large dining-room for a meal which was served upon fine porcelain decorated with the Blythe crest. The set had been in storage for nearly two decades, Lady Cavender told Miranda, and it was intact.

"I've managed to engage a few servants, but once you're installed here you may wish to import some from town, or rely upon the registry office at Bath. In the morning I'll show you the rest of the house, while Justin is busy with the bailiff." She beamed at her son, seated at the opposite end of the long table. "Nick and Nerissa have offered themselves as dinner guests tomorrow night, but beyond that I have planned nothing."

"Does my uncle join us?" he enquired as he carved a slice of roast beef for his betrothed.

"An attack of gout keeps him in Bath, but he hopes you and Lady Miranda will call in Camden Place. Now Elizabeth," she said to the duchess, "you must relate all the news of your family. I trust your younger son has come through all these Peninsular battles unscathed?"

The ladies embarked upon an amiable colloquy, and Justin turned to Miranda. "What do you think of this old pile?" he wanted to know.

"It is so beautiful," she replied in a voice of awe.

"And sadly neglected. I was a schoolboy when I last dined at this board, and Ram sat here—he had just inherited. Now this chair is mine, and yet I feel as if it isn't, not really."

After dinner Lady Cavender led the way to the chamber she had chosen as her drawing-room when she'd come to the house as a bride. "You'll find that very few of the apartments are truly comfortable," she told Miranda. "I've given you and your aunt the least daunting of the bedchambers. So much needs be done to make this barrack a home again. Though I had the desire, I lacked money enough, and I spent my married life trying to economise as best I could."

She pointed out the harpischord to Miranda and invited her to try it. "I remember hearing you play at Haberdine, when my brother and I stayed there the year of your come-out. I thought then how happy I should be to have a young woman like you for a daughter-in-law."

Miranda had always liked Lady Cavender, with whom she was already acquainted, but had not realised how much she doted upon Justin. Her ladyship's eyes shone with love and pride when he told of his involvement in the negotiations with Persia, and she encouraged him to explain to her just why Lord Castlereagh and Mr. Canning had quarrelled. Her questions revealed how slight was her understanding of politics, but she was eager to discuss anything that was important to her son.

It had been a long and tiring day, and Miranda tumbled into her unfamiliar bed expecting to drop off almost at once. As she did, she wondered whether she ought to receive her own guests in the drawing-room or the larger salon.

In the morning the pleasant fumes of wood smoke teased her awake. Someone had already kindled a fire and left a tray on the table beside her bed, and as Miranda leaned against her pillows sipping the hot beverage, she admired the flower-printed Chinese silk lining the walls. There was a water stain near the window, and she made a mental note to discover whether any of the leftover material was stored in some attic or lumber-room. Possibly the section could be replaced, saving the expense of re-hanging the entire room.

After breakfast the master of Cavender Chase departed for the stable and the duchess went outside to look over the gardens. Lady Cavender took Miranda on a tour of the house which took the better part of the day. They began in the state apartments, magnificent by any standard.

"What a perfect setting for a ball!" Miranda exclaimed when they entered the *salon des glaces*, an enormous chamber panelled from ceiling to floor with gilt-framed mirrors.

"The inspiration for this room, more than any other, was Louis the Fourteenth's palace at Versailles," the viscountess told her. "Come, you've not seen the library. Dominic Blythe says it's a perfect disgrace, so few volumes have been added of late years." After showing off the whole of the ground floor, she took Miranda upstairs where the principal bedchambers were situated.

As they moved from room to room, Lady Cavender spoke in the quiet, purposeful way which reminded Miranda of Justin. "Never fear that I begrudge you taking my place here, and you needn't worry that I shall interfere in the management of the house. I've never been partial to the Chase—it's too large and formal for my taste, and too few of my memories are happy ones. I'm no more than a Sussex baronet's daughter myself, and Fairdown, my father's house, did not prepare me for such grandeur. But you were bred at Swanborough Abbey and raised at Haberdine Castle and will not be so amazed."

"On the contrary," Miranda said with a smile, "I am very much amazed."

"I do hope you won't be as lonely as I was when I first came here. I had not been wed long when I sent for my sister Celesta to be my companion—that's how she happened to meet and marry Beau Lovell. A handsome man, but without warmth or any softness in him. Those who say Damon is like his father are greatly mistaken."

"I am not one of his detractors," Miranda said staunchly.

"The two families have been here forever," Lady Cavender informed her. "The Blythes live north of the river and the Lovells to the south of it. I'm afraid the local tenantry have suffered from their landlords' absence. Elston Towers has been as much neglected as the Chase, and with less cause. As you are no doubt aware, my nephew never visits Wiltshire. He lived the early part of his boyhood here, and as you may know, it wasn't a happy one, either before or after his parents died."

She went on to name some of the other families of the district, concluding, "And then there are the Lansdownes at Bowood, but my husband had a falling out with the first marquis and it was never mended."

When Miranda had seen the whole of the establishment from garret to cellars, she was more confused than enlightened. Lady Cavender said she would soon learn her way, but Miranda was doubtful, and that night at dinner she asked Justin to draw her a map of the house, not altogether in jest.

"I couldn't even if I wanted, for trust me, I know my way round only a little better than you. And maybe not as well."

His reply amused their guests, and Dominic Blythe said merrily, "You must remember to tie a string to Lady

Mira's wrist every time you go out so you may be sure of finding her upon your return!"

There was more laughter, and when it died out his lordship's wife heaved a sigh. "If only we could lure Damon back to the shire, how happy we would all be together!"

Miranda couldn't imagine why Nerissa's wistful remark should have displeased Justin, but immediately afterwards he retreated into silence and solemnity.

Would they turn out to be as well-suited as their cousins seemed? She envied Nerissa, whose beautiful, expressive face radiated contentment. Never had she imagined that the wild Miss Newby could settle so comfortably into wedlock. Fate had been kind, providing her with a mate as handsome and passionate and scandalous as she, and one who was very nearly as rich. The Blythes had met entirely by chance, and Miranda knew she and Justin had been brought together by design, but for some time she had been of the opinion that Mr. Isaac Meriden possessed talent as a matchmaker.

Justin drove her to Bath one afternoon to call upon his uncle, who showed Miranda the many treasures he had collected in India and presented her with a small statue of the Hindu mother-goddess Parvati, for luck. It was made of gold, with sapphires for eyes and ruby-studded lips, and Miranda supposed it must be a very valuable piece.

Her week in the country slipped away, and with each passing day she felt increasingly optimistic about her future. Two days before they were to return to London, Justin invited her to join him in a walk around the park, saying she'd spent so much time indoors that she'd had no opportunity to explore the grounds. During their stroll he recounted the details of his latest conference with his remaining tenants and detailed the improvements he had already set in motion.

"The outbuildings are in good repair, but I must put the vacant cottages in some kind of order if I wish to attract good people to the farms. My bailiff has done the best he can, but he has grown old for the job. As soon as we return to London I must seek out a man more knowledgeable about modern methods of farming."

"What were you and Lord Blythe discusing so long last night after dinner?" Miranda enquired.

"I made him an offer for some Southdown ewes. He said it was too high, and we wrangled over that until I convinced him I could well afford the price."

"But that's backwards bargaining!"

"So said Nick." Gesturing towards the graceful does grazing in the shade of an ancient oak, he said, "You see what pets we've made of our deer, though they used to run wild here. There has been hunting at the Chase since the time of the Tudors, and very likely before. Nick told me many a fox wants killing. He assumed the management of the Blythe kennels years ago and finds the whole business a damned nuisance. He's more interested in farming, and last night he gave me quite a lecture on the damage the local huntsman did to his fields last winter." Smiling down at Miranda, he told her, "Compared to what you've experienced at Swanborough Abbey, what passes for sport here may seem tame, but I remember some deuced fine runs when I was a lad!"

He returned to the problem of how to make Cavender Chase profitable as quickly as possible. She need not be concerned that he would use her money to purchase items which could be made upon the estate, nor had he any intention of filling his stables with bloodstock. Somewhat to her surprise, she realised that she didn't mind how much of her fortune went into improving the property; during the past week she had learned to regard it as her own.

She said as much to him, adding, "I really have no home. Though I was born at Swanborough Abbey, it belongs to my brother. I was almost twelve when I went to live at Haberdine, but it is a Marchant house and I am a Peverel. Ninian and I are the last of our father's family."

"But your mother is living."

"To me it's as if she were dead. From the little I've heard of her, I think she might as well be."

Facing her, he reached out to place his hand upon her shoulder. "How can you judge, Miranda, knowing so few of the facts? Surely you'd prefer to hear the truth," he persisted, "rather than accept lies which have been circulating so long they pass for fact. You aunt told me you never ask about your mother, and I can't believe you are disinterested."

"Justin, please." She brushed him off impatiently and walked on.

"Your uncle visits Bath from time to time, and he told me himself that he writes Lady Swanborough regularly to give her news of you and Ninian. You might do the same."

Miranda turned to face him. "Do you mean write to her, or . . . or visit her?"

"Both, if you wished." He led her over to a dead tree which had been felled, and when they were seated upon the broad trunk he told her of his conversation with her aunt, before they had left London.

"Do you mean you discussed my feelings, plotted behind my back? Oh, Justin, how *could* you?" she cried. "You have no right to interfere."

"Not even the right of someone who wants to see you completely at peace?"

"You think my paying a duty visit to a madwoman will accomplish that?" Her face registered horrour. "You must have guessed I would refuse!"

"No," he said soberly, "I knew nothing. In all the time we've known one another you've only mentioned her a few times, and always with pain. I think it a great pity that you should deny her existence, but I am not forcing you to go to Bath. Your aunt says, and I agree, that the decision must be yours." He leaned forward and printed a light kiss upon her brow. Climbing to his feet, he told her he was going back to the house. "I will leave you alone to consider what you should do. I'm sorry if you think I overstepped myself—I meant it for the best."

Miranda drew a long, ragged breath and watched him

walk across the park, his brown head bowed. His figure grew smaller and smaller as she sat there, dazed, her mind boiling with questions.

Her mother was forever enshrined in her memory as the beautiful, weeping creature she had known during her childhood. In the years since she had gone to live with her aunt and uncle, she had grown familiar with the graceful contours of a pale, oval face, much like her own, in the Romney portrait hanging in the Castle gallery, and the famed Hoppner canvas at Solway House. But she had ever been careful to think of that person in the abstract; to do otherwise was to be haunted by alarming visions of a shock-haired, screeching lunatic.

Abruptly she rose from the tree trunk and set out across the damp and springy turf, walking in the direction of the church. What should she do? The frantic question echoed with every footfall. She loved her mother ... and feared her almost as much.

The churchyard where Justin's ancestors slumbered beneath ancient oaks was silent and peaceful. Wandering among the headstones, she read the names and the flowery inscriptions extolling the virtues of the Blythes who lay at her feet. A monument marking the newest grave was bare of all but a name, a familiar one. Ramsey Blythe, her former suitor, had lain there for over a year, yet until now she hadn't quite accepted the fact that he was gone. All this time it had been as if he were still living out his lonely exile. Whereas her own mother, still very much alive, seemed entirely dead to her. The unfairness of it struck her, and she was ashamed. Mad or not, Lady Swanborough must still be capable of maternal affections; she would surely remember and might even miss the daughter she had left a decade ago.

Miranda looked towards the house and saw Justin on the front steps, waiting for her and worrying about her. He had given her a choice and trusted her to make the right one. She could not disappoint him—or herself— and on that thought she picked up her skirts and hurried across the lawn to tell him so.

Justin pulled the horse to a stop in front of the terrace of houses called the Paragon, and Miranda hopped down before he could come around to assist her. He left the gig in the care of a boy standing by the curb, and when Miranda had smoothed the creases from her white muslin gown and retied her straw hat for the second time since leaving Cavender Chase, they approached the house. Although she was pale, when he lifted the doorknocker she gave him a small, off-center smile.

Mrs. Mostyn, a homely woman of middle age, ushered them inside. "The doctor will receive your ladyship in his study," she said, leading them down a corridor. "So untidy it is," she fussed, "and he won't let me in to clean it proper."

Her husband's chamber lived up to its reputation, and all surfaces were obscured by books, papers, and ledgers. Dr. Mostyn came out from behind a large leather-topped desk to shake hands with his visitors. Of medium height, he had dark hair going grey at the temples and piercing dark eyes. After clearing two chairs, he invited Justin and Miranda to be seated. "Mrs. Mostyn keeps one of the front rooms in readiness for callers," he said, "though I seldom make use of it. During a consultation I must sometimes refer to notes or one of my texts." His voice was low and soothing; an accent betrayed his Welsh origins.

Miranda sat tongue-tied while Justin thanked the doctor for seeing them.

"It is my pleasure," he replied. "Lady Swanborough has long been my patient, and by virtue of her living in my home she takes precedence over all the others." Fixing his intens gaze upon Miranda, he said, "I will enlighten your ladyship as best I can, for Lord Cavender has told me some of your concerns. First of all, there is no evidence that Lady Swanborough's affliction is the sort which tends to run in families."

She turned accusing eyes upon the one who had exposed her hidden fear.

Dr. Mostyn continued, "When I received word that you would be coming today, I told Lady Swanborough, and her pleasure is beyond description. Ever since her recovery she—"

"Recovery?" Miranda interrupted. "Dr. Mostyn, do you mean to say that she's no longer ill?" The doctor's nod confirmed it. "But . . . is it possible to cure madness?"

"That has been true in His Majesty's case, though we may not have a perfect understanding of how. Dr. Willis, most unfortunately, has refused to publish his methods and principles of curing lunatics, but others have achieved similar success. I could tell you of instances even more remarkable, where there has been no recurrence of derangement." He smiled and said in his calming way, "Lady Swanborough has been well for the past two years, but she will always suffer from a nervous disorder—one of the neuroses, as Professor Cullen of Edinburgh has named them. They are not perfectly understood at present, but that does not preclude their being successfully treated. If such a corollary existed, not a doctor among us would have a practice."

"If my mother is not now ill, why is she still confined?"

"She doesn't consider herself to be, as you will learn when you've spoken with her."

"Yes, of course. May I do so now?"

Dr. Mostyn led her out of the cluttered room and up a staircase, but he paused on the landing. "You will find Lady Swanborough in the second room on the right."

"Won't you come with me?" she asked, alarmed.

"It is better that you go alone."

She hesitated but he smiled and nodded encouragingly, so she proceeded along the hallway towards a door which was slightly ajar. When she placed her hot, moist hand upon the brass knob, she recoiled at its coolness.

The room was bright; her first impression was of sunlight and white-painted walls. The Countess of Swanborough, seated on a sofa, was sewing a piece of yellow cloth so long that several yards of it trailed across the floor. Her hair, once as black and shiny as a raven's wing, was dull and streaked with silver, but it was still arranged in the simple, loose coiffure of the Romney painting.

Miranda, uncertain of the welcome she would receive, dipped a tentative curtsey. "Good day, my lady."

Her mother looked up, and Miranda couldn't see if she smiled or frowned because her own eyes were flooded with tears. They obscured her vision, and she walked blindly forward until she felt a pair of thin arms close around her. "So pretty," Lady Swanborough wept. "I never imagined you could be so very pretty."

As Miranda dried her mother's damp cheeks with her own handkerchief, she saw that time had etched fine lines around the drooping mouth and the eyes of Marchant blue. "Was I such a plain child?" she asked.

"Oh, no, only it startled me to see you grown into a young woman, looking as you do . . . as I once did. And now you are going to be married." She picked up the length of yellow silk and held it up so Miranda could see the pattern of embroidered flowers and butterflies. "I've made this counterpane as your wedding gift."

Miranda touched it reverently. "Such exquisite work— it's almost a tapestry."

"Soon it will be finished and I shall begin the bed curtains. I'm afraid they will take rather longer."

"Do you spend all day sewing?" Miranda asked.

"I read also," her ladyship replied. "And I have my own carriage. Three days a week I go out for an airing, usually to Widcombe or Chalcot, and on Sundays I attend divine service. I stay away from public gatherings, but sometimes the musicians from the Assembly Rooms come here to play for me. Though I live quietly, I am not at all bored."

"But if you are so well, why must you remain with Dr. Mostyn? Uncle William would be happy to have you live at Haberdine."

"I told him what I must explain to you, Miranda. I am far better off as I am. You need not feel sorry for me, either. I have my own rooms, all of them as pleasant as this one, and a servant, old Matilda Bleaklow. Another lady has come to live here, so I have companionship when I want it." After a brief pause, Lady Swanborough aid, "The last time I seemed to be restored to health, I suffered a recurrence of my illness—it was agony. You have heard of that, I'm sure."

"Yes," Miranda admitted. "I don't know what happened. I always wondered but was afraid to ask."

"I was out shopping by myself, something I used to do on my good days," Lady Swanborough said in a quiet voice. "I was standing in a haberdasher's shop sorting through some white lace on a table—Nottingham lace. I remember it perfectly clearly, though what happened afterwards has always been a blur. All at once I felt that I was about to break into a thousand pieces, as though I were made of glass—a sensation I used to experience frequently in crowded or noisy places, yet never so painfully as then. When I cried out for help, everyone looked at me so strangely. As I became more and more agitated I forgot who I was or how I had come to be there, but one lady recognised me and sent for Dr. Mostyn. I recall nothing of what happened afterwards—my delusion lasted for a week or more. Bath being what it is, the incident was much talked about, and the gossips embellished it until the talk bore little resemblance to the truth."

As she sat there holding her mother's pale, blue-veined hand, Miranda regretted the stubborn fear which had kept them apart for so many years. "I wish I'd known," she said unhappily. "I ought to have come sooner."

"I was beyond comfort, child. I prefer that you know me as I am, not as I was. The affliction which impaired my mind has amended, but in truth it was madness which long held me in its grip. And only by continuing this regular, restricted mode of living can I hope to keep well." Lady Swanborough toyed with the embroidery spread across her lap. "And how fares my little son?"

"He is hearty, but not even the strictest of the masters at Harrow has quelled his naughtiness."

Her mother's thin shoulders lifted in a sigh. "He deserves better by way of a mother, poor lamb. But your uncle tells me Elizabeth spoils him. I would never have predicted that, she was so strict with her own boys."

On impulse, Miranda asked, "Would you like to come to my wedding? It's to be New Year's Eve, and the family will gather at Haberdine for Christmas. I'm sure Justin—Lord Cavender—would want you to be there as much as I do."

Lady Swanborough shook her head and said gently, "It would be too difficult for me, the long journey, the excitement of the occasion . . . seeing Ninian. But we shall meet again, I trust, when you are settled at Cavender Chase."

Miranda's face brightened. "Indeed, you must come to visit us. And when Ninian has his holidays, he will come, too, and then you shall see him again."

She did not stay much longer, for she fancied her mother was not quite up to long visits. They parted, each promising to write, and Miranda kissed her ladyship's soft, ivory cheek before dropping the respectful curtsey which etiquette demanded.

Justin waited for her in Dr. Mostyn's study and in response to his questioning look, she gave him a tremulous but joyful smile.

On their way back to Cavender Chase she tried to express her feelings. "I can scarcely believe I have seen her and touched her and talked with her. She's not at all what I imagined. In a way she's almost like a child, so gentle and subdued, and yet she seems a thousand years old. There's something in her eyes. Not sadness exactly, but a *remembered* pain."

Shifting the reins to one hand, Justin encircled her waist with his free arm. "I look forward to meeting her, but I couldn't insist upon it today. Will she be at Haberdine to see us married?"

Miranda shook her head. "But she does want to stay with us at Cavender Chase. I'm sure she would feel comfortable there, as it's quiet and secluded." She turned to him and said, "I'm sorry for being so beastly yesterday.

You are wise and kind and patient and altogether wonderful, and I wish my fortune were ten times its size, for you deserve that, and more."

"And I'm glad it isn't, or I'd never be able to convince you I had other reasons for chasing after you," he said, and Miranda was inclined to believe he had spoken from the heart.

=10=

THE PREPARATIONS FOR the Jubilee had begun by the time Justin and Miranda returned to London. The government might seem on the verge of collapse, and the war had dragged on interminably, but there would be a great celebration to honour the fiftieth year of His Majesty's reign, for only two previous monarchs had ruled so long. Jubilee songs had been composed, pamphlets chronicling the king's life were circulated, poems were written extolling his and England's virtues. By royal proclamation, all deserters from the army and navy were to be pardoned; persons imprisoned for small debt were released and benevolent societies raised subscriptions to pay off their creditors.

The twenty-fifth of October would be a day of pleasure for Miranda. She and Justin were going to see the transparencies on display in Piccadilly and Ludgate Hill, and later there would be a royal fête at Frogmore, Her Majesty's house. She had seen more of Mr. Lawrence and her dressmaker than of her fiancé since her return from Wiltshire, but now her bride-clothes were fitted and her portrait sittings nearly at an end. In a few weeks she and the Marchants would depart for Northamptonshire, and there she would remain until the day of her wedding.

Justin was late, but he had a ready explanation: his cousin had returned. "Now that the rightful master of Elston House is in residence, I've reverted to my former lowly status. His arrival caused such an uproar belowstairs that the servant forgot to bring my shaving water at the usual time."

"Why didn't you invite Damon to join our expedition?" she asked, pulling on her gloves.

"He was weary," Justin said curtly. "Do we walk, or have you ordered a carriage?"

"It's only a step to Piccadilly, let's walk. We can always take a hackney into the city."

"A hackney?"

"The truth is," she confided, "I've never ridden in one, would you mind?"

"Not in the least. My whole object is to provide you with amusement."

They found a crowd standing in front of Stubb's shop, where three painted canvas transparencies were on display. The largest was twenty feet square and depicted the king in his coronation robes seated upon the throne.

The window of Rundell and Bridge featured a more elaborate representation of the monarch, and included several more life-sized figures: Wisdom in a helmet carrying a spear, Justice with her scales and sword, Fortitude standing beside a pillar, and Piety holding a Bible. A willowy female was shown adorning a pair of columns with oak garlands and medallions engraved with the victories won by the army, and her counterpart paid the same honour to successful naval battles.

Justin's suggestion that they go inside the shop found favour with Miranda; she liked to browse even though she had no intention of buying any of the expensive wares filling the cases. Mr. John Bridge himself came forward to assist them, and with his most obsequious bow, he asked how he could be of service.

"I wish to purchase a gift for her ladyship, some token of the Jubilee," Justin announced.

"Certainly. If you will come with me," the gentleman said, bowing again.

"That fellow has an exceedingly flexible spine," Justin murmured in Miranda's ear as they followed him to another part of the shop.

She doubted that anything in the shop could be had cheaply, and when Mr. Bridge brought out a velvet-lined tray of jewellery, she said under her breath, "Really, you mustn't. I've already got a souvenir. Uncle William gave me a Jubilee medal."

The tray removed for Lord Cavender's inspection contained a collection of brooches, rings, and seals with the king's likeness, and other assorted trinkets. Holding up a pair of gold ear-drops set with a ruby, a sapphire, and a tear-shaped pearl, Mr. Bridge pointed out the colours of the Union Jack.

When they exited the shop, Miranda carried a small box in her reticule. "The earrings match my costume for the royal fête," she told Justin, "though you shouldn't have bought them." They paused at the curb and he looked about for a hackney to carry them back to May-fair. "There's one," she said, pointing out a dilapidated vehicle across the way.

Justin, seeing that there was no other vehicle in sight, signalled to a boy to sweep a crossing. The coach looked even worse at close range, but it was the only one, so he handed Miranda in and gave the jarvey the direction. A moment later they were bowling westward along the Strand at a furious pace.

"I wouldn't have guessed those poor horses were capable of such speed," Miranda said as the hackney dipped and swayed. "Can you make him drive more slowly?"

Justin pounded the roof with his walking stick, but the man on the box failed to respond in the desired fashion.

"Open the window and shout at him," she suggested, poised between panic and a fit of the giggles.

"I can't, the damned window is stuck," he said impatiently. She covered her mouth with her gloved hand to smother a laugh, and he grinned. "You see what comes of such recklessness. I should think the fellow is drunk—we'll be lucky not to be killed." The coach rocked dizzily to one side and he flung a protective arm around Miranda.

"What on earth," she gasped, greatly shaken.

"We've just managed to avoid colliding with Saint

Clement's Church," Justin reported. Looking away from the window, he saw that her bonnet was wildly askew. "I fear your feather is broken."

"At least it wasn't my head," she said, more giddy from being held so close to him than from the swaying carriage. She leaned against him brazenly, and her hope that he might kiss her was instantly fulfilled.

Justin drew back to say, "This is precisely why properly brought up young ladies are warned never to ride alone in closed carriages with young gentlemen."

"Do you mean to cry off, now that you know what a daring creature I am?"

"On the contrary," he replied, "it only makes me wish our wedding were not two months off." His mouth claimed hers once more.

All too soon the hackney deposited the dishevelled couple at the corner of Park Lane and Mount Street, and Justin was so much pleased by the results of the wild ride that he neglected to take the jarvey to task. He saw Miranda to the door but said he dare not come inside lest the duchess ask what mischief he'd been up to. "I do wish, though," he said, his brown eyes gleaming with humour, "that Lawrence might paint you as you are now. You look delightfully wicked."

He kissed her hand, then turned and walked back to Elston House as beatifically and effortlessly as if he were borne upon a cloud.

That evening Miranda, like most people attending His Majesty's fête, was dressed in the colours of the Jubilee, and with her velvet gown of garter blue she wore a crimson scarf draped about her shoulders, and her new eardrops. As she paraded with her aunt and uncle along the grounds of Frogmore, she received a civil bow from the frail, consumptive Princess Amelia, the king's youngest and dearest daughter, who appeared briefly on the balcony.

Her eyes raked the crowd for Justin's tall, lean figure, and she soon saw him making his way towards her, another lady at his side.

"I have a great fear of brigands," Princess Levaskov said, removing her hand from Justin's arm long enough to shake Miranda's, "so I begged his lordship's escort from town. Lady Miranda, had you a pleasant stay at the Chase?"

Miranda, stung by the familiarity with which this woman, a virtual stranger, bandied the name of her future home, made an effort to reply civilly. The Russian lady had not conformed to the prescribed colours: her dress was lilac, very becoming, and she wore a Turkish shawl so large that it trailed upon the grass like a train. Miranda's dislike intensified on being quizzed in flawless French, but she responded in kind.

"Such a pity that the war is on," Natasha said, "and the English cannot visit Paris to improve their accents."

Nettled by what she deemed a criticism, Miranda said that she had been taught French by a native of Normandy.

"And what other languages have you, Lady Mira?"

"Just my own, Princess, but I sing in both Italian and German."

"You will be amazed, for I am not at all clever, but I am fluent in six languages—Russian, German, French, Swedish, Italian, and English. As a child I spoke Polish, for my father had estates in that country, but my mother thought it not genteel." She flashed a cat-like smile and added, "Lord Cavender says I would make a most suitable wife for a diplomat."

Miranda's cheeks went scarlet to match her tippet, and she stifled a most unbecoming retort. "Admired Miranda," someone hailed her, and she turned to see Lord Elston standing there.

"Damon," she said in relief, clutching his hand as though it were a lifeline.

"I must felicitate you, *chérie*, but I am also fortunate. Before long mine will be the honour of addressing you as cousin."

His familiar drawl fell pleasantly upon her ears, and she was struck by how handsome he was in a frock coat of Windsor blue with large gilt buttons. Smiling up at him, she said, "How I've missed you! Are you fixed in London?"

"Until I join you at Haberdine for all the fun."

She managed to produce a laugh, but it was only a faint echo of the one his banter generally elicited, and her smile was fleeting.

"Why so long a face on this day of celebration?" he asked, cocking his golden head.

She shrugged dismissively, but her friend was not deceived; drawing her apart from the others, he bade her tell him what troubled her. "Princess Levaskov," she answered in a voice no less savage for being kept to a near-whisper.

Damon looked upon the Russian lady through narrowed eyes. "What the devil is *she* doing in England?"

"Do you know something about her—him—them?" When he failed to reply at once, she begged him to tell her the truth.

"Be easy, *chérie*, I know nothing. I shouldn't think you have anything to fear. She's an enticing creature, but no beauty."

Miranda said bitterly, "You rub the wound when you should apply the plaster."

"When did she arrive?"

"I'm not perfectly sure, I was still in Brighton. She has a son at Harrow; he and Ninian have become fast friends. There's another child, a baby, but I've never seen him."

"Well, let us hope her motherly duties will keep her out of Justin's way," he said grimly, thereby fanning the flame of Miranda's fear. He stayed by her side for the rest of the evening but his attentions, rather than comforting her, had the opposite effect. Something was very wrong; he had realised it, too, and he was trying to protect her.

The guests massed around the lake to view the water pageant, which was less than a complete success. Damon let Miranda have his quizzing glass, and she held it up to her eye to observe the mechanical sea horses as they pulled two chariots bearing Britannia and Neptune across the the water. Four smaller boats followed, each filled with persons intended to be tritons and mermaids, but the choristers who were supposed to sing "God Save the King" were unable to reach their places, the crowd was so vast.

Illuminations followed, signalling the end of the spectacle. By that time Miranda's head had begun to ache, for her velvet gown was uncomfortably heavy and she was tired of watching the princess cling to Justin's sleeve. As the volleys of rockets burst overhead, she remembered the Prince of Wales's birthday, and how passionately Justin had kissed her on the lawn of the Marine Pavilion at Brighton. Had it been folly to accept his offer? Although she had forgiven him for choosing her as a way to repair his fortunes, she could not forget it, especially now that he sought the company of another woman. It occurred to her that Princess Levaskov must have known of his need to wed an English fortune; perhaps they had agreed she would follow him as soon as he accomplished his mission. Miranda dared not confront him with her suspicions, nor did she wish to leave London with so many questions unanswered.

At the end of October Lord Granville wrote to Justin from Chiswick, announcing his engagement to Lady Harriet Cavendish. The Duke of Devonshire had approved the match, and his lordship hoped that all his friends would share in his joy. Justin did, but as he folded up the note, he couldn't help wondering how the Countess of Bessborough would receive the news.

Justin was not so busy preparing for the Persian ambassador that he neglected Miranda, but he was unable to haunt Solway House as he had done before receiving his assignment. He took tea there a few afternoons each week, but he seldom saw her of an evening. Whenever they met he was conscious of constraint on her side; he set it down to natural agitation as their wedding day drew nearer. Whatever her fears or concerns, she did not share them.

It had not escaped him that her manner had begun to

change at about the time of his cousin's return. If his own best efforts had not erased Damon's golden image from her heart and mind, there was nothing else he could do but accept the situation and hope they would be discreet. After the wedding he would take care to keep his bride safe from temptation by keeping her at Cavender Chase; he deemed it fortunate that Damon avoided Wiltshire as assiduously as if it were plague-ridden.

But for now Lord Elston escorted Lady Miranda Peverel about town, and at night they danced together in the ballrooms of Mayfair. Justin, kept busy at all hours by politicians and ministers, might not have heard about it had Natasha not shattered his blissful ignorance.

"Of course," she said during one of his visits to her house in Brook Street, "the marquis is so attractive and quite the flirt. I suppose he cannot help having the ladies chase him a little."

"As to that, I should think it's Damon who does the chasing," Justin said grimly. It was a rainy November evening, and as he gazed out of her parlour window he could see the pavements glistening in the lamplight. "Lady Miranda's sense of propriety is too great, she would hardly encourage a gentleman's attentions when she is already engaged."

"Lady Pembroke did tell me that people are beginning to talk. Since coming here I know the favourite English sport is not fox-hunting at all, but gossip."

He could not deny it. But he doubted his ability to halt what he convinced himself was no more than a habitual and essentially harmless flirtation. Miranda continued to talk of their future together as if nothing were amiss; her aunt and uncle treated him as one of their family.

On the eve of their departure for Northamptonshire, Justin called at Solway House to bid Miranda farewell and found Damon there. As a consequence, the parting scene was neither as private nor as tender as he had envisioned it.

"This snowfall will make your journey a tedious one," he said a trifle stiffly, uncomfortably aware of his cousin's interested presence. He fancied there were hollows beneath Miranda's cheekbones; her eyes seemed larger than ever and faintly shadowed. "I'm sorry I cannot go with you, but the *Formidable* has docked at Plymouth. The Foreign Office received word by telegraph last night."

"You needn't apologise. For the present, your duty is to the Persian ambassador."

"But only until Christmas," he reminded her. "And after the first of the year I will be entirely yours."

"You ought to have that put in writing," Damon advised Miranda. "Is it too late to add it to the marriage contracts?"

"The papers have been drawn up . . . *and* signed," Justin said, without attempting to mask the note of triumph. Looking at Miranda, he added, "In the eyes of the law you and I are already bound, though we haven't exchanged our vows."

"I'm not learned enough, nor have I the energy to debate the points of spiritual and civil law," she replied in a subdued voice.

"I hope our Mira will benefit from country air," Damon commented. "London is so dismal at this season, with these fogs and foul humours."

Justin, goaded beyond the limit of his endurance, said sharply, "I never thought to hear you recommend ruralisation, Damon."

"I am so much a convert that I'm contemplating a winter visit to Wiltshire," Damon replied, his voice like silk. "But I'll take care to keep away from Cavender Chase during the honey-month." He flashed his most mocking smile.

Justin had to content himself with kissing his fiancée chastely upon the cheek, and as he stepped out into the dark and gloom of late afternoon, he wished he might throttle his cousin.

The day after Miranda left London, he accompanied Mr. Charles Vaughn, Mr. Arbuthnot, and some others from the Foreign Office to Hertfordshire to meet Mirza Abul Hassan Kahn, the newly arrived emissary from Persia.

The Persian and his white-gowned servants awaited the British deputation in his private parlour at Demezy's Inn, and he was an exotic figure in his turban and floor-length robe of rich embroidered silk. His eyes were black and brilliant, his mouth full and red, but the lower part of his swarthy face was obscured by a black beard. Mr. Morier, who had accompanied him from Persia, shook hands with his countrymen, who welcomed him back to England.

Abul Hassan, he explained, did not yet speak English fluently, so he would be acting as interpreter, and his first duty in that capacity was to express the Persian's delight with the elegant state coach the government had sent to carry him into London.

Justin and the other gentlemen spent the evening at Demezy's, listening to Abul Hassan's favourable impressions of Bath, where he had stopped on his journey from Plymouth. In the morning the English diplomats returned to the capital in their own carriage; Abul Hassan and Mr. Morier rode in the coach of state followed by two stagecoaches bearing a retinue of servants. The procession did not halt until it reached the handsome residence in Mansfield Street allotted to the foreign envoy for the duration of his visit.

When the weary and curiously despondent Abul Hassan retired, Mr. Morier reported to Justin that the Persian gentleman was much distressed that the downpour had prevented a welcoming crowd from meeting him. "As we drew near the city, he made me cover the windows of his carriage to hide his shame. He said it was as if we were smuggling contraband into London rather than receiving an envoy from the most royal of princes. In his country," the interpreter explained, "important visitors are met by an *istekbal*, a large party headed by some gentleman of distinction bearing gifts."

"I hope you informed him that no disrespect was intended," said Justin.

"Oh, I did, I did." Mr. Morier wagged his balding head. "He thought I was only making excuses for his being slighted."

The following day being Wednesday, the king made his weekly pilgrimage from Windsor Castle to Buckingham House, where he met with his ministers and bestowed the seals of the office of foreign secretary upon the Marquis Wellesley. Justin spent the morning in Downing Street; that afternoon he called upon Abul Hassan and found him pleased by Lord Wellesley's promotion. The marquis, he had heard, spoke Persian as well as Arabic and Turkish, and must therefore be a most superior person.

With Mr. Morier's assistance, Justin told Abul Hassan that Sir Gore Ousley was his official host. "But his house lies outside London, so he was not able to wait upon you last night. In his absence I am to carry out any of Your Excellency's wishes."

It was too soon for Abul Hassan to have any particular desires, and although Sir Gore's failure to wait upon him was a fresh cause for dissatisfaction, he was cheered by a visit from Lord Radstock, a relation of Mr. Morier's, and later in the day Sir Gore arrived. Abul Hassan's face lit up when the grey-haired baronet addressed him in his own language, welcoming him to England on behalf of the king and the prime minister. The black eyes sparkled with tears, and when he had mastered his emotions he began to speak.

"He says," Mr. Morier whispered to Justin, "that his host's Persian is so fluent that he doubts he is truly an Englishman. It is his hope that God will be good enough to allow this fine man to become ambassador to Persia someday, for none could be better suited to the position."

Abul Hassan was so charmed by Sir Gore that Justin had no qualms about leaving them together. He returned to the Foreign Office to report these events, then hurried to Elston House to write an even more detailed account to Miranda.

On Thursday he visited Mansfield Street again; Sir Gore had not yet removed from the country and would be unable to attend the Persian envoy until the evening. Abul Hassan, now settled into his new abode, made a request, and through Mr. Morier he said, "I require a supply of rice for my native dishes. And I would wish to have live animals and game birds brought here for my servants to slaughter themselves, for they are not used to purchasing livestock already killed."

Justin, carefully preserving his countenance lest he offend, assured Abul Hassan that the livestock and rice would be forthcoming. He departed, with no intention of returning for a day or two, but that evening his leisure was interrupted by an urgent summons from Sir Gore.

He called for a carriage and hurried to Marylebone and Abul Hassan's house. When he entered the salon, the baronet rushed to his side, his face and voice expressive of grave concern. "Our minister of protocol desires a translation of the shah's message to the king, but His Excellency Abul Hassan tells me one was already sent from Persia. Moreover, he refuses to unseal the letter he has brought with him and says it must be delivered intact into the king's hand."

Justin found himself at a loss. "But I can't make an appointment for him to see His Majesty," he said, shaking his head. "Why, the ambassador from Constantinople has been waiting over three months for his audience, and the gentlemen from India and Russia and a host of other countries have all but given up." He contracted his brow, trying to come up with some way to put off the insistent Persian. "Remind him that our English customs are different. Say that he must rest from the long voyage, and that we will be happy to show him the sights of London to help him pass the time until he receives a royal summons."

When this proposition was put to Abul Hassan, there was another angry outburst.

Sir Gore said hopelessly, "He refuses to set foot outside this house until he has seen the king."

For the rest of the week Justin worked hard to placate his determined charge, and he sent urgent messages to Mr. Perceval, imploring him to make an exception in the case of the Persian minister and to smooth his way to a meeting with His Majesty. Abul Hassan was convinced that if he did not carry out his duties in a timely fashion, the wrath of the shah would fall upon his head. By day Justin went back and forth from Downing Street to Marylebone, bearing messages and reassurances; at night he and Sir Gore danced attendance upon Abul Hassan. The baronet organised music parties for the envoy's entertainment and brought the world to Mansfield Street, for Abul Hassan would not stir beyond his front door. When he fell ill of a fever, Justin supposed its cause was sheer frustration.

"And homesickness," sighed Sir Gore, who had grown fond of the stubborn foreigner. "He misses his own country very much."

On Monday of the following week the new foreign secretary tried to pour oil on troubled waters by calling on the Persian envoy. Lord Wellesley and his attendants came in ceremonial dress as a compliment, and Abul Hassan was curious about the ribbons and orders which decorated the chests of the delegation.

Said the marquis, with a pleasant smile, "I regret that you didn't come to our country in a better season. In winter the sun turns its face from the city, and day becomes as night."

Abul Hassan pointed to the medal pinned to the foreign secretary's breast, a sun embossed with the royal seal, and made a comment in his own language. Sir Gore Ousley stepped forward to translate. "In London's darkness the sun won't shine. Stand upon the roof, my lord, with *thine*."

"Bravo, bravo," said Lord Wellesley, and a host of diplomats breathed a uniform sigh of relief.

It was not long before the prime minister followed his foreign secretary's example. Mr. Perceval called, bringing Lord Harrowby and some welcome news for Abul Hassan; the day of the royal audience was fixed. The king would receive the shah's envoy at Buckingham House on the following Wednesday.

When Abul Hassan expressed sadness over the delay, the prime minister told him that His Majesty was old and ill. "And every day which passes is to me a lifetime," he replied sadly. "I must beg you for a letter to His Majesty the Shahanshah, Hope of the Incomparable God the Creator, explaining this delay. He will be most displeased and blame me for my prolonged absence from his court."

After a brief consultation with Lord Harrowby, Mr. Perceval said, "It shall be done."

On the long-awaited day, when Justin informed Abul Hassan that the prime minister had written the requested letter, he said fervently, "God be thanked that my life will not be forfeit!"

A state coach drawn by six bay horses had been sent to carry him to his audience, and this splendid equipage had drawn a crowd which ran the length of Mansfield Street. Abul Hassan climbed inside, followed by several of his own attendants, and Justin nodded to the liveried coachman. The people began to cheer, and as the carriage moved forward large snowflakes began to fall.

When Justin next saw Abul Hassan, he was a new man: smiling, cheerful, and eager to talk of his presentation.

"The king was dressed in royal robes. I took the gold casket containing the shah's letter and placed it in his hands. He gave it to the prime minister and enquired about the health of my esteemed ruler. I assured His Majesty of the shah's friendship and affection and begged that he would assist us in removing the Russians from our city of Tiflis. This he promised to do if he could."

Sir Gore smiled and said, "Your Excellency has left out His Majesty's compliments to you. Lord Cavender, he said that no other monarch had sent him so young and learned an ambassador, and it speaks to the glory of the Shah of Persia."

"My lord," Abul Hassan said in English, "now that I have been permitted to fulfill my duty, I must see the sights of London!"

=11=

FOR CENTURIES HABERDINE CASTLE had sat like a crown atop
a hill which commended a view of three shires. A royal
fortress from the time of William the Conqueror, it had
been purchased from the crown by a Marchant enriched
by the Tudors. His son had made improvements with a
lavish hand, never guessing the house would again serve
its intended purpose, but during the civil wars it had
been a Royalist stronghold. The gate towers and thick
outer wall had withstood repeated attack, but the castle
keep was greatly damaged and had been pulled down
and the stones used for the chapel in which Miranda
would be married on the last day of the year.

Accompanied by her groom, Tom, she spent many an
hour on horseback. One morning she set out for Swanborough Abbey, following the ancient track which had
connected the local villages—Great Melden and its
pretty Norman church, the collection of thatch-covered
stone cottages which was Little Melden, and Stoke Saint
Matthew, with the horsepond where her cousins Gervase
and Edgar had often bathed with their friends.

When she had departed the district to try her fate in
London, the grass had been richly green and damp with
the rains of early spring, and the golden heads of the
daffodils had nodded farewell to her. Now the hillsides
were coated with frost, and a carpet of fallen leaves was
spread upon the ground. Soon it would be time to gather
the holly and mistletoe: Christmas was but a few days

away, and in little more than a week she would be married.

Hearing the familiar, piercing horn blast from the valley, she guided her mare into a clearing in the hope of glimpsing the huntsmen. Her uncle did not ride out any longer, citing his health, but he was still the chief patron of the Swanborough hunt, which met twice a week.

"There they are, m'lady."

Miranda shielded her eyes from the sun and followed the direction of Tom's outflung arm until she saw the hounds, followed by the galloping steeds ridden by gentlemen in scarlet coats. "They're making for that old covert where we always found the fox last year," she observed. She picked out her cousin Gervase's crop-tailed bay and envied him; it was a morning made for hunting. "After the frost, the scent will be running high," she sighed.

"Mayhap, m'lady, but with so much fallen leaf, it won't lie well in cover," was her companion's sage comment as they rode on.

The wooded path skirted the banks of a small lake, and its waters shimmered in the morning. Miranda spied a heron standing statue-still among the dry reeds just before it spread its wings and flew slowly over the trees and out of sight, on its way to a less public fishing place. At last she caught sight of her birthplace, and she reined in for a long look. Swanborough Abbey incorporated the remains of a Benedictine convent granted to the Peverels after the Dissolution, and it had once quartered the same soldiers who had assaulted Haberdine in the time of Cromwell.

The stable yard was crowded and bustling, a certain sign that the hounds were running. Bow-legged grooms were saddling their masters' second horses; younger boys clad in Swanborough hunt livery shovelled muck. There were a few horse-jobbers lurking about in the expectation of selling off a slug of an animal to any sprig of fashion who had run a favourite mount off its legs. Miranda, feeling the hard, calculating eyes of those men upon her, was not inclined to linger. When she dismounted, she walked past the stables to the famous modern structures which sheltered the Swanborough pack.

The youth who swabbed the sloping, brick-paved courtyard ceased his task for a respectful tug at his cap. When the kennel-feeder emerged from the first building with his pail, he waved to Miranda. "Good morning, Webb," she greeted him. "I trust I've come in good time to see you feed the hounds."

The old man's lined and weathered face was lit by a smile. "Aye, and your ladyship is welcome to stir the barley if you've a mind."

She went with him to the feeding yard, where a giant copper containing boiled oatmeal had already been set out. Webb emptied the contents of his pail into it and gave Miranda a wooden paddle with which she stirred the thick, viscous mixture.

"I tell you, my lady, it's a chore to keep the second pack in equal flesh," Webb grumbled when the hounds, nearly eighty in number, were let into the yard by his assistant. "But they're good ones, they are," he said proudly as a swarm of dogs gathered at the trough to lap up their warm mash. "You're looking at the best, handiest lot of youngsters I've ever had in my keeping. Bluster there," he said, gesturing at one dog with the knob of his whip, "came back t'other day with a thorn in his pad. Caliban has sore feet . . . I've been soaking them in brine since he was last out. And a couple of 'em are lame in the knees. Ho, there, Brawler, look to your own trough!" he admonished one greedy individual.

When the hounds had satisfied their appetites, Webb let them into the grass court. "We'd heard as how all the grand company was expected at the Castle soon." He slapped his coiled whip against his thigh. "I well remember Lord Cavender's father, and his poor brother, rest his soul—now there was one who sat well upon a horse. It's pleased I am that your ladyship will wed into a hunting family."

His approval of the match amused Miranda, as did his amasement when she told him Lord Cavender had lately hunted wolves in Russia.

Swanborough Abbey at hunting time was hardly a suitable retreat for a young lady, as the housekeeper took it upon herself to remind Miranda. After assuring the woman that she would be on her way before the gentlemen returned, she explained she'd come to collect something of her mother's to wear at the wedding, and thus gained entrance to the countess's old rooms. The furniture was shrouded with holland-cloth and the curtains drawn, but she spent the rest of the morning there, sifting through chests and lifting trunk lids in search of a scrap of lace or some long-forgotten trinket to wear. Nothing of much value remained. She did find some white satin rosettes, now yellow with age, and a pair of narrow-toed, high-heeled shoes with paste buckles. When Miranda slipped them on she found that they were a perfect fit, and regretted that they were out of fashion and therefore useless.

Undaunted, she continued her search. In one drawer she came across a packet of letters tied with a faded ribbon; several pairs of kidskin gloves, cracked and stiffened by time; and some of the tall plumes which had been so fashionable in the decade of her birth. Buried beneath these, wrapped in silver paper, was a piece of Mechlin lace. Its only flaw was a musty smell from being shut away so many years, but Agnes would know some way to freshen it. Miranda carefully replaced the paper around her discovery and carried it belowstairs.

She and Webb returned to the Castle while an enormous travelling carriage was being divested of its baggage. Miranda's hope that Justin had arrived was dashed by the stable boy, who told her it had come from Bath.

"You're sure it wasn't London?" she asked him.

"Aye, m'lady. 'Twas full of fine-dressed folk. Two ladies, one young and one not, a baron, and a gentleman with a face as yellow as a duck's foot were riding inside. There was a maid and an India-man riding on the dickey."

This description of the Blythes, Lady Cavender, and Mr. Meriden sent Miranda hurrying inside, and she found them all in the timber-vaulted hall, recruiting their energies with tea.

"What a charming habit!" Nerissa exclaimed. "Have you been hunting?"

Lord Blythe gave a husky chuckle. "She would hardly be back so early if that were the case, Nerissa."

"Unless she only rode over the first few fields," Isaac Meriden interjected. The duchess, pouring out a cup for her niece, said she had discouraged Miranda from hunting this year. "I should think so," the nabob huffed as he passed a handkerchief over his sallow face. "Can't run the risk of a broken neck so close to the wedding day!"

"I only rode as far as Swanborough and back—very sedately," Miranda told them. "Tom will vouch for me."

When she finished her tea she went up to change, accompanied by her cousin. As they entered her room, Nerissa said worriedly, "Lady Cavender and I have but one woman between us. I hope we shan't need to dress terribly fine."

"Never mind, Haberdine has more servants than you can count, and Agnes will take special care of you," Miranda assured her. "Did you leave my godson behind?"

"We had no room for him, small as he is," she replied, going to a mirror to smooth her unruly chestnut hair. "Nick is glad to have me all to himself for a while, and our nurse is trustworthy and devoted to Dickon. Now where are all your new things? I long to see them."

Miranda invited her to look through the two wardrobes containing dresses for all occasions: muslins and cambric and figured chintz for day wear, walking costumes, a new riding habit, and several ballgowns, including one of gold satin. Nerissa sighed over an elegant pelisse trimmed with fur and as she stroked its velvet sleeve she expressed her envy of so well-endowed a bride.

"I didn't go to my husband with half as many clothes. Is this for the wedding?" she asked when she came to a gown of white satin embroidered with silver thread. "How beautiful you'll be. I shall weep my eyes out, I know it. And where are your gifts?"

Miranda led her across the hall to a wainscotted parlour to view the many offerings which had poured in from all parts of the country, and jumbled though they were, they made a magnificent display. Additional tables had been brought in and were heaped with china and silver and boxes of jewellery. She showed off an amethyst brooch from Gervase and the pretty gold and pearl bracelets sent by Miss Berry and Miss Agnes. She had received inkstands in abundance, and a superfluity of candlesticks. Mr. and Mrs. Canning had provided a writing case, and the good wishes of the king and queen were represented by a splendid gold tray.

"Look at this," she said, taking up a small case of tooled leather. "There's a travelling clock inside, from Lord Hartington. His sister sent this tea caddy, and Lord Granville that vase. They are also marrying this month."

Nerissa wandered to another part of the room to examine a silver-handled riding whip. "What thoughtful person provided you with this?"

"The stable staff, organised by Tom, my groom—isn't it dear of him? And Richards gave me a set of silver spoons. He says in his experience, no household can ever have enough of them!"

Out of consideration for the travellers, the duchess ordered dinner to be served early, and afterwards the company repaired to the drawing-room. The four ladies played whist while the gentlemen discussed hunting, in which the duke and his old friend Meriden continued to take an interest despite their retirement from it. Gervase, an attractive young man with his mother's fine grey eyes, described the performance of the Swanborough hounds; his seniors listened avidly, and the baron with amused civility.

When a footman entered to announce the appearance of a carriage in the drive, Mr. Meriden said confidently. "That will be Justin."

Nerissa looked up from her cards to say, "Mira ought to be the first to welcome him."

Her face pink, Miranda left the room. Richards had

just admitted a tall, cloaked figure, and she forced herself to walk calmly along the hall. The gentleman removed his hat, uncovering a halo of golden hair. Then he stepped aside, revealing a diminutive person whose face was partly obscured by a hobgoblin's mask. The apparition let out a fearsome growl and Miranda shrieked in pretended alarm.

As her brother ran past her to terrourise a footman, she greeted Damon. "How did you acquire Ninian? My uncle's chaplain, Mr. Penfield, was going to fetch him later this week."

"Harrow was not so far out of my way," her friend replied. "His lordship and I had a most interesting journey together, and he only cost me a small fortune in cakes and pies along the way." He shook his head and intoned, "A devil, a born devil."

"I know," she laughed, "and it was very kind of you to bring him. Is Justin paying off the postboys?" She cast a hopeful glace towards the front door, then looked back at Damon in time to see his fleeting frown. "He isn't with you?" she wailed.

"Mira, those chaps at the Foreign Office have ordered him to show some black-bearded infidel all over London."

"But he *will* be here for Christmas. Won't he?"

"Sir Gore Somebody's wife is ill, and it has fallen to Justin to entertain the Persian. That's all I know," he said testily.

It was her second great disappointment of the day, for two carriages had come and neither had brought Justin. But she couldn't be angry, knowing it was duty which kept him from her side, and she was certain his efforts would prove him worthy of some advantageous diplomatic post.

Christmas dawned blustery and cold. In the morning the Marchants and their guests shivered through divine service in the chapel, then gathered before a roaring fire in the library. The older ladies settled down to piquet and gossip at the card table. Ninian challenged his sister and cousin Nerissa to a game of snapdragon, at which he excelled, and quickly defeated them. Nerissa then retired to a corner with a book; her husband went with Damon and Gervase to the billiard room. The duke and Mr. Meriden were occupied in passing the London papers back and forth, and Miranda managed to seize one.

She spread it open on the sofa, starved for town news, and although Ninian tried to break her concentration by marching his toy soldiers across the page, she was impervious. Affronted, he stalked off, leaving her in peace. She lingered over a page devoted to matters theatrical, and read that Covent Garden playhouse had reopened now that Mr. Kemble, bowing to mob pressure, had reinstated the old price of three shillings and sixpence for seats in the pit. The charge for boxes was still high, seven shillings, and as a result the actor had been hissed during his performance last week. After perusing the account of the uproar at Covent Garden, she moved on to a review of the new comedy presented by the Drury Lane Company at the Lyceum. A number of eminent persons had attended the debut of Mr. Cobb's play *Sudden Arrivals or, Too Busy By Half*, among them Viscount Cavender and Princess Natalia Levaskov.

Far too busy by half, she fumed, and with that Russian widow rather than the Persian envoy!

"What's made *you* so skittish?" Damon asked her later when he intercepted her beneath a kissing bough of mistletoe bound with red ribbon. "You're still a free woman . . . for another week."

Seven whole days, she thought in despair. How would she ever survive them, burdened by suspicion as she was? "I must save my kisses for your cousin," she replied, then wondered what difference it made. Apparently he wasn't saving any for her.

"I caught you, *chérie*," he teased, "and by right I can demand any forfeit I wish."

Her sense of fair play compelled her to submit. When his lips grazed her cheek, she remained composed and detached, for Damon had never really touched her heart.

Was it because he had never tried to, or because she demanded too much, more than he could ever offer? There was a kind of love between them but no passion. Yet he was here, snatching kisses, while Justin, whom she loved to distraction, was consorting with another female.

"Take care how you encourage Damon," Nerissa whispered to her that night. "What would Justin say if he knew his cousin was bussing you in hidden alcoves?"

"It was only a bit of holiday funning. My old life has ended already but the new one hasn't quite begun . . . Did you feel troubled and unsure just before you and Lord Blythe were married?"

"I scarcely remember," Nerissa answered. "Nick and I were wed in a sadly harum-scarum fashion, everything happened so quickly that I never had the opportunity to consider or reflect." In a more thoughtful vein, she continued, "It was after the ceremony that my doubts surfaced."

Miranda regarded her cousin curiously. It occurred to her that neither Nerissa nor Dominic had ever discussed their wedding, or stated exactly when or where it had taken place, and the mystery of it intrigued her. Though she was reluctant to curtail this interesting conversation, she saw Lord Blythe hovering nearby and gave her place to him.

Damon, violin in hand, called for her to join him in a duet. As she made her way to the pianoforte she glanced back at the sofa and saw the baron reach out to smooth back a strand of his wife's hair. The tenderness and intimacy of his gesture cut Miranda to the quick. Would Justin ever look at her as if she were his whole world, she wondered, or was she destined to compete for his attention with foreign diplomats and lady foreigners?

Justin spent his Christmas at Abul Hassan's house in Mansfield Street wishing he were at Haberdine Castle. He could imagine the gaiety and good cheer he was missing: the parlour games, the singing of carols, the wassail and claret cup. Instead, he provided companionship to a member of another faith who had no appreciation for the holiday and was pining for his native country. Abul Hassan's lack of spirits was also due to the foreign secretary's failure to call upon him.

"But it's Christmas," Justin said again when Abul Hassan wondered for the tenth time what prevented his lordship from coming, as he had promised to do.

"This excuse is unacceptable," said the Persian. "I will write to Lord Wellesley to tell him of my displeasure. I wonder why he hides from me when he knows my only desire is to make stronger the ties between our two nations. His most noble majesty the shah commanded me not to remain in London more than forty days. Almost thirty have gone by and still the treaty terms are not agreed upon."

Before leaving the house, Justin said they would call at Apsley House tomorrow night on their way to the opera.

In his precise, clipped English, Abul Hassan stated his disapproval of this plan, saying, "I do not think it would be correct to go to a theatre from the house of your most illustrious foreign minister."

"As you wish," a weary Justin replied.

He put on his hat and greatcoat and stepped outside, pausing uncertainly on the pavement when he realised there was no place he wanted to go. Elston House was a tomb; most of the servants had been given leave by their master and the rest were making merry below-stairs. Turning up his collar, he stepped into the waiting carriage. From Marylebone to Mayfair, he passed the brightly illuminated windows of persons more fortunate than himself, and the dark and empty ones of the closed shops. By the time he reached Brook Street he was feeling so lonely that he sought the only solace available to him.

Natasha was delighted to see him, as always. This year, she said, she was having two Christmases: first the English one, then another twelve days hence, according to the Russian calendar. Feodor was home from Harrow, eager to tell of his progress there, and while Justin listened he dandled little Ivan on his knee.

"I had not expected you to be still in London," Natasha commented when her son finished describing the awful punishment the headmaster had inflicted upon Lord Swanborough. "Did you not tell me, on the night we went to the play, that you would go to the duke's castle as soon as might be?"

"I should be there now," he admitted. "But Sir Gore Ousley's time belongs to his lady, who hasn't recovered from her illness, and all the junior ministers are with their families, or out of town. The task of amusing Abul Hassan has fallen to me."

She gave a gurgling laugh. "He would rather have other company, I think. At the assembly at Lord Radstock's house, did he not say he was tired of talking only to men and old women, and that his taste ran to young ladies?"

"Poor Hassan, he spends every waking hour in fear that the shah will have his head if he lingers too long."

He regaled her with a few choice anecdotes about his Persian friend, and she expressed her admiration of his cleverness in handling so exacting a visitor. Justin ceased to watch the clock, and before he knew it the nurse came to remove Prince Ivan to the nursery and Feodor was sent off to his dinner. Natasha invited her visitor to dine with her; this being preferable to another solitary meal at Elston House, he accepted.

His contentment and his comfort were impaired during the dessert course when she raised the subject of his forthcoming journey to Northamptonshire. "My own coach is very fast," she told him proudly. "If you wish, we might travel together to Haberdine Castle."

Justin knew not how to answer her. It was evident that she fully expected to attend his wedding, although he'd never given her any reason to believe he wanted her there. After a moment of indecision, he realised he could not repay her hospitality by insulting her, but as he nodded his head he wondered what the devil Miranda's relatives would think when he arrived with an uninvited guest.

Natasha dimpled at him. "I shall await your convenience. Feo will stay with my cousin until he goes back to Harrow. But Ivanushka must come with us, for Agatha is so stupid I must keep my eye upon her always. You do not object? The motion of the carriage makes him sleep, he will not be a trouble." She drank a mouthful of soup, then said, "Now tell me, *mon cher*, have you received letters from the Lady Miranda?"

"Not lately, but I suspect she has been very busy. The Castle is filled to the rafters with company."

"And Lord Elston will have arrived," Natasha said significantly.

"I daresay he's spending his time chasing foxes," Justin replied, trying to believe it himself.

"Ah, I was remembering today what happened a year ago this time, when you went wolf-hunting with my brother. Do you recall also?"

"I'm hardly likely to forget it," he said absently.

"My pains began as soon as you had left Droskoe, and there I was, alone but for the servants. You and Nikolai came home to find Ivanushka arrived."

Justin listened to her reminiscences with only half an ear. He envied Granville, who had managed his marriage with very little fuss yesterday at Chiswick.

Justin wished he had not acquiesced so readily when his superiors, who knew the date of his wedding as well as he did, had requested that he look after Abul Hassan. He'd been so intent on proving his merits that he'd raised no demur, and too late he recognised what he should have done. Tomorrow, he told himself, he would call in Downing Street to sever his chains, and then he could make his way to Northamptonshire and his neglected bride. He didn't care what the diplomatic staff would think; as far as he was concerned, the gentlemen of the Foreign Office could go and hang themselves.

He had already sacrificed too much to ambition. Knowing only too well the rewards of success in his chosen profession, his innate honesty forced him to acknowledge that they no longer appealed to him. If in future he should be posted to some foreign, far-off court as envoy or ambassador, he must choose between leaving his wife behind or dragging her along with him. And he wasn't even sure that he wanted to be sent abroad again. He'd seen quite enough of the world, more than most men dreamed of, and putting Cavender Chase in order would be task enough for one lifetime.

His impatience to begin was such that he spent Boxing Day closeted in the library of Elston House with his bailiff's report. That evening, when he escorted Abul Hassan and Sir Gore Ousley to Apsley House, his mood was ebullient. While Abul Hassan admired their host's Venetian mirrors and French paintings and Irish crystal chandeliers, Justin counted the hours until he would see Miranda again.

Lord Wellesley greeted the Persian envoy with a high degree of respect, promised to speed the process of negotiation along as best he could. Much of the ensuing conversation was critical of Russia, so Justin held his tongue and kept his opinions to himself, for he was still a partisan of that country and its misguided emperor in spite of the alliance with Napoleon. He was so quiet that he attracted the attention of Lord Wellesley, who regarded him speculatively for the space of several seconds before saying, "Our government intends to send an ambassador of distinction to Persia in order to strengthen the bonds of friendship between the exalted shah and our king."

The foreign secretary said nothing more, but this was sufficient to give Justin a clue to his lordship's thoughts, and he judged it sadly ironic that he should be deemed worthy of so desirable a mission only hours after deciding to relinquish his budding career as a diplomat.

Abul Hassan's voice filled the silence. "My lord, the customs of Persia are very different from those of European countries. It is ruled directly by the shah, the shadow of God on earth; it has no council of ministers. Your English ambassador would meet with our most holy ruler and therefore must not only be a man of accomplishments but also a linguist. Interpreters only hamper the forging of friendships between nations."

Justin recognised that Abul Hassan was tactfully pointing out that Gore Ousley was the natural and obvious choice to undertake the job of pacifying the shah of Persia. He mentally applauded his foresight in neglecting to study Persian and expressed his agreement with Abul Hassan. To his surprise, he felt no real regret about removing himself from consideration.

When the Persian envoy's audience with Lord Wellesley was over, he and the others were taken into a room where food and drink had been laid out. Several gentlemen were there, among them Henry Wellesley, recently chosen to replace his brother the marquis as ambassador to Spain.

"What the devil are you doing here, Cavender?" he cried. "I thought you were off somewhere being married!"

"Not until the week's end," Justin said cheerfully. "I leave town tomorrow."

Mr. Wellesley, whose experience of matrimony had been notoriously bad, shook his head. "I wish you all the best. As a divorced man, or nearly that, I can't give you any advice, except to say be wary of any gentlemen who appears to fancy your wife."

=12=

JUSTIN'S DESIRE TO leave London immediately was thwarted by Natasha's extensive and, to his mind, excessive preparation. He had hoped to travel to Northamptonshire on the twenty-seventh, but it was not until the following day that the carriage bearing him, the princess, her son, his nurse, and the baggage set out. Bad weather forced a halt at Bedford, where they stopped for the night, and after a late start on the twenty-ninth, they resumed their journey, reaching Haberdine Castle late in the afternoon.

Richards showed them to the library, where they found the company being entertained by the antics of a pair of unruly foxhounds. Miranda was seated on the low leather hassock with her brother, their black heads close together. Looking towards the door, she gave Justin a warm and welcoming smile which faded when her eyes swept past him to rest upon his sable-cloaked companion.

The Duchess of Solway claimed his attention first, and he said under his breath, "I hope the addition of another guest won't be an inconvenience."

"If I told you the number of people we can sleep at the Castle, you wouldn't credit it. I think we had better turn the rooms in the west wing over to your guest and her entourage," the duchess concluded as she caught sight of the nurse and the baby.

"Princess Levaskov brought her linen with her, as is the custom in Russia," Justin explained. "I tried to persuade her there was no need."

"Visitors to Haberdine are encouraged to do whatever makes them most comfortable," said the duchess, and he gave her a relieved smile, thinking she would make an admirable diplomat.

He was desperate to speak to Miranda but had to wade through a vast crowd to get to her. He kissed his mother, shook hands with his uncle and the duke, nodded at Gervase, and exchanged civilities with Dominic and Nerissa. Just before he reached his beloved, her little brother accosted him.

"The foxhounds are my wedding present to you and Mira," Ninian announced. "She says you've got a small pack in Wiltshire, and I thought your stock might want improving. They are called Dainty and Delicate, and their sire was Dragon, the most famous of all our Swanborough dogs."

One hound came forward to greet her new master, who took hold of the soft muzzle. Even to Justin's untutored eye, she looked well-proportioned, with straight legs and an erect tail. "Who is this?" he asked.

"Delicate. You can tell by the white patch on her side. You missed the hunt on Boxing Day," the boy informed him.

"But there's another tomorrow," said Miranda, who looked like a flower in her rose-coloured gown. Justin felt a surge of emotion so strong that his heart throbbed and his head swam; the clamour of all the other voices seemed to fade.

"I'm sorry to be so long in coming," he told her.

"Damon explained how busy you've been," she replied, and there was a coolness in her tone. "He has ridden over to Belvoir to call upon the Duke and Duchess of Rutland, but he'll be back for his dinner." In her worst imaginings she had not anticipated having her rival introduced into her wedding party, and when Princess Levaskov came forward, hand extended, she could barely contain her outrage. "Had you a pleasant time at the theatre the other evening?" she asked. "I read in the paper that you and Lord Cavender attended the comedy at the Lyceum."

Natasha blinked, as if taken aback by such directness.

"It was *forte amusante,* and I had much enjoyment from the English actors, though our Russian players are excellent. Lord Cavender knows, for he often escorted me to the theatre in Moscow, when we stayed at my townhouse there."

The cat-like smile which accompanied this speech struck Miranda as retaliatory.

"I was amazed," the princess went on, "to see how the English ladies receive their gallants in their boxes, and the husbands sit with their mistresses."

"You paint a dismal picture of our society," said Justin wryly.

Why had Princess Levaskov come to Haberdine? It was a question Miranda could not ask, for she didn't want to communicate how very frightened she was. She wondered if the others were conscious of the awkwardness of the situation; perhaps, like her, they were pretending to accept the Russian's presence because their breeding demanded it. And she received the princess's gift—a set of glass sherbet cups in silver stands—with a plausible imitation of gratitude.

By the time she went upstairs to change, her spirits were so low that she let Agnes convince her to wear a gown she did not like very much, a figured sarsnet. When she went down to the great hall, where the family generally met before proceeding into the dining-room, she found the princess there before her, the picture of exotic elegance in crimson velvet and her necklace of opals.

"Ah, Lady Miranda," Natasha purred, "I have another little offering, more intimate than the sherbet cups." She removed an agate ring from her right hand and pressed it into Miranda's palm. "Here is a token of the esteem I feel for you, the lady soon to become the wife of my dear Lord Cavender. I hope with *tout mon coeur* that you and I shall be friends."

This overture set the seal on Miranda's dislike and mistrust; she was nettled, as always, by the other woman's proprietary air whenever she spoke of Justin.

The chime of the dinner bell put an end to her ordeal.

The guests began to descend the staircase in twos and threes, and for once the rules of precedence worked in her favour. When they went in to dinner, her uncle escorted Princess Levaskov, Damon went in with the duchess, and Gervase offered his arm to Lady Cavender. Ninian, who outranked Justin, dined in the nursery, so the engaged couple entered the dining-room together, as did Lord and Lady Blythe. Mr. Meriden, the only commoner, brought up the rear.

During the first course Natasha observed, "Here the custom of dining is much the same as in my own country, quite formal. But at our dinner parties, the best food is placed at the head of the table where sits the host, and those persons seated far away from him receive the dishes that are not so fine. The English way is more . . . more . . ."

"Democratic," Justin supplied, and everyone laughed.

When the cloth was removed, the duchess and her female guests retired to the drawing-room *en masse.* As they passed beneath the gallery, a youthful voice pleaded from above, "Mayn't I come down, just for a *little* while?"

"No, Ninian, you may not," the duchess answered. "It is nearly ten o'clock, and high time you were abed."

"But I haven't bade Mira good-night yet. Or Lord Cavender . . . or Damon or Ger."

In response to her aunt's look of entreaty, Miranda intervened. "If you don't go to bed now, you'll be kept home from tomorrow's hunt." Her statement had the desired effect, and Lord Swanborough withdrew.

At the duchess's request, Miranda sat down at the pianoforte to play a few selections from her repertoire. When she was done, Nerissa said, "It is a sore trial to me that I lack the accomplishments deemed so necessary in polite society. You, Mira, are fortunate to possess them in abundance. And I overheard Cousin William telling Mr. Meriden that you act as his secretary and help him to write his speeches."

She understood: Nerissa was giving her the opportunity to show off before the princess. "He composes them himself, I merely copy them out," she said, closing the instrument.

"What an unusual ring," Nerissa commented later, when Miranda brought her teacup. "I noticed it while you were playing. From Justin?" Miranda explained that the agate was a gift from the princess. "I must say, her coming here uninvited is the *oddest* thing, for I know well enough that only the families were asked. I wonder if she means to follow her cousin's example and marry into the English peerage. Gervase is a bit young for her, though heir to a dukedom, or she might be laying snares for Damon. Ought we to warn her that it's a hopeless cause?"

"I can't guess her motive," Miranda said frankly. "You can never tell who's really your friend, and she seems rather too eager to be mine."

The Russian lady's constant references to her native land, resulting in comparisons which were unflattering to England had long grated on Miranda. Soon the unwelcome guest was describing the vast properties she had inherited from her father.

"The emperor told Prince Paul he had good fortune to win me," Natasha said, toying with the ends of her gold-spangled shawl. "When I married I had over fifty thousand peasants."

Miranda was provoked into retorting, "I prefer having a dowry reckoned in pounds and shillings, rather than human souls."

A tense silence fell but was immediately broken when Nerissa, with an aplomb that the duchess might have envied, complimented the princess on so handsome a babe as Prince Ivan. Natasha, ever ready to talk of her children, beamed with maternal pride. Nerissa informed her that she, too, had a little boy, and the young mothers embarked on a lively discussion from which Miranda, childless, was excluded, and glad of it.

Early the next morning the young gentlemen of the party assembled in the castle courtyard to quaff a cordial before setting out for the Swanborough Abbey meet.

"Nerissa tells me you rolled the little Russian up quite neatly last night," Dominic Blythe told Miranda when she handed him his stirrup-cup.

"If I did," she said, stroking his horse's smooth neck, "I shouldn't have tried. I behaved very badly."

She moved on past Ninian and his pony to perform the same office for Justin, mounted on Gervase's bay, and presented him with a silver vessel in the shape of a fox-hound's head. After reading the Swanborough hunt motto engraved upon the collar, he looked down at her and asked, "May I see you alone when I return? It's important that I speak to you."

Miranda had despaired of ever having such soft intimacy in his voice, and casting her eyes upwards, she saw that he was smiling. "We might meet before tea."

"In private," he repeated.

"If you like."

"I've a confession to make," he told her, gathering up his reins, "and I warn you in advance that I depend upon your forgiveness and understanding."

When he looked at her like that she could not think, and only after the horsemen vanished through the tower gates did his words register with her. As she went into breakfast, she told herself that his transgression could not be so very bad; he had been too cheerful. And because Princess Levaskov ate breakfast in her bedchamber, Miranda was spared her disruptive presence at the table.

She spent that day, her last as a single woman, quietly. After she had read aloud to her uncle for an hour, he told her how much he was going to miss her, although he wished her happy with his whole heart and was sure she would be. "Your portrait arrived from London today by carrier. Originally I intended to hang it here, with George Romney's painting of your mother, but I've changed my mind. I want Lord Cavender to have it." When he saw her fumble for her handkerchief, he said in a hearty voice, "What's this, little Mira? You mustn't cry. As your aunt would say, it gives the most dreadful impression. I thought you wanted this marriage."

"Oh, I do, it's just that you are so good to me, and I can't quite believe I'm being married tomorrow."

After clearing his throat, the duke said uncomfortably, "You have nothing to fear from Lord Cavender, but if you're concerned about . . . about anything, you had better talk with the duchess, or Nerissa."

Laughing through her tears, she said, "I didn't mean *that*, Uncle, honestly. Besides, I've already talked to Nerissa—Aunt Elizabeth, too."

"Good, good." He patted her shoulder awkwardly. "Now don't go telling Cavender about the portrait, for I mean to present it to him this evening, after dinner. Elston will no doubt try and persuade him that the canvas should be exhibited at the Royal Academy in the spring, but if you don't like the idea, you have only to say so."

When Miranda went to the library to pen a letter to her mother, she found Justin and Dominic at a table, still in hunting garb, their heads bent over a map. Nerissa was stretched out upon a sofa with an open book. "Here you are," she said, "just when you're wanted. You know this country well, as Nick and Justin do not, so please tell them which would be the preferred route to Cavender Chase."

"Whichever one brought you here, I should think."

"If only it were that simple," Nerissa sighed, assuming a more lady-like position to make room for Miranda. "Nick has decided that it won't do, as you and Justin aren't breaking your journey. He thinks there must be some more direct road."

"Nerissa," her husband called, "did you know we're very near to Lutterworth?"

"Are we?" She blushed, for no apparent reason, and resumed her reading.

"Have you ever been there?" Miranda asked. "It's an ordinary little village, nothing out of the common."

With a glanced at his wife's bowed head, Dominic replied, "Once we were there, several years ago, and can recommend the Denbigh Arms as an ideal resting spot, especially for a new-married couple. Be sure to ask Mr. Frank for his best bedchamber."

"Really, Nick, the things you say," Nerissa admonished him, her face still aflame.

Miranda could tell from the way Justin smiled that he was party to the secret, whatever it was. Shaking his head, he told his cousin, "Your inn won't do for us, Nick. I'm determined to press on to Cavender Chase, even if it takes all day and night."

"I expect it will," Nerissa observed. "What a stubborn race is that of Blythe!"

Being in the company of the Blythes went further in relieving Miranda of the worries which had beset her. In future they would enjoy many such afternoons, at Blythe or Cavender Chase; they were neighbors, and their children would be playmates.

But her contentment was shattered when Princess Levaskov entered the room. She carried her son in her arms, and with a helpless smile, she presented the wriggling bundle of white lawn and lace to Justin. "He has just come awake and is *trés exigéante*," she said by way of explanation.

"It is always so," Nerissa remarked in the voice of experience.

Justin placed the child on his knee and bounced him until he chortled, and said, "You see why I am so handy with your Dickon."

Miranda thought Prince Ivan comely enough, but not nearly as taking as her godson. His hair was brown and straight and he had dark eyes, but he was too young to much resemble his brother Feodor, or his mother.

When Nerissa asked if she might hold him, Justin handed the boy to her. The princess wanted to know if the gentlemen had enjoyed their morning, and Miranda expected a dissertation on the superiority of the Russian wolf over the English fox. Gathering together the pen and paper she had come for, she left the library.

Hearing the click of the balls coming from the room across the hall, she peeked inside and saw Damon bent over the billiard table aiming a shot. "Hullo there," she said, and he glanced towards the door. "I'd counted on you to be the life and soul of this party, and you've failed me. Why have you kept to yourself so much?"

He gave her a long, assessing look. "I admire your fortitude, not to mention your self-control, but if I were in your shoes, I'd turn Justin out of doors, wedding or no." He let his stick fly and waited for the ball to fall into the pocket before speaking again. "The woman is a barbarian to come here at such a time. Even the Countess of Bessborough had the delicacy to stay away from Chiswick when Granville wed Lady Harriet Cavendish."

Miranda's blood ran cold at the confirmation of the fear which had gnawed at her ever since the princess had crossed the threshold of Haberdine. "Then she *was* his mistress," she breathed.

"Lord, yes, the whole world knows it. Including the bride."

"Not Lady Bessborough," she choked. "Princess Levaskov."

"I don't know what she is, but I'm fairly certain she came to England thinking Justin would marry her." He walked around the table and examined the position of the balls.

At that moment Miranda remembered her brief exchange with Justin early in the day. "Dear God," she whispered, "he means to tell me. He wishes to make a confession, and he said he relies upon my understanding. It must mean that their *affaire* is not over. What can I do?" she wondered aloud. "If her hold on him is so strong that she induced him to have her at the wedding, my position is weaker than I thought." She couldn't deceive herself; faced with the truth, she had to accept it.

"Demand that he give her up," was Damon's advice.

"Oh, I couldn't," she said, horrified at the thought of such a confrontation. "Wives don't. *Do* they?"

He shrugged. "Don't ask me. But really, you needn't make a martyr of yourself. Tomorrow morning my cousin is going to make all manner of promises to you, and it's within your rights to demand that he keep them."

He had a point. But what he suggested went against

everything she'd heard on the subject of marital infidelity. A female was expected to turn a blind eye to her husband's amours.

Dreading a repetition of the night before, with its undercurrents and tension and intrigue, she watched Justin and the princess throughout dinner for signs of collusion, some visible proof of their sinister confederacy.

Afterwards, in the drawing-room, the ladies talked of weddings.

"I scarce remember mine, it was so long ago," said Lady Cavender. "I was a little afraid of my husband's relations—he had a vast number of terrifying aunts."

"My marriage day was certainly memorable," the duchess declared. "Nerissa's father was the duke's groomsman, and he came to the ceremony in a state of inebriation. Poor Richard . . . I couldn't be angry, for he'd just lost his wife, whom he adored. After he went back to sea he became quite steady again."

Miranda waited for Nerissa to tell her tale, but although her cousin smiled, as if amused by her memories, she did not speak.

"In Russia . . ." the princess began, but the fatal words died on her lips, for the gentlemen were coming in.

A footman followed, carrying the painting by Mr. Lawrence, and the duke presented it to Justin. The half-length portrait was, everyone agreed, a perfect likeness, and its recipient declared himself enchanted.

Only Damon failed to given an opinion, although he said silkily, "Lucky fellow, to possess both the copy *and* the original."

The servant took the canvas away to be properly packed for the journey to Wiltshire. Miranda perceived that the princess, who delighted in being the center of attention, was jealous; the carmined lips pursed in annoyance, but then they smiled. "Do come and sit with me, Lady Mira," she said, patting the cushion of the settee invitingly.

Miranda's instinct warned her that the other woman would try to discomfit her, and she resolved not to succumb. When asked how long she and Justin would stay at Cavender Chase, she said coolly, "Until Parliament convenes, I expect."

"I hope his lordship will not be long away from London," the princess sighed, "for I depend upon his visits to cheer me. I have begun to feel homesick, and he was in Russia for so long that sometimes I forget he is not of my country. When all these hostilities are settled, as they will surely be, I pray that your king will appoint him ambassador to the Court of St. Petersburg."

Miranda, thinking that nothing could be more disagreeable for her, said that it was a trifle soon for Justin to expect such an honour.

"I once wished my sons to be soldiers," Natasha continued, "but now I think they must be diplomats, like milord. You have met my Feodor, have you not? And you must know of Lord Cavender's fondness for Ivanushka. It is natural, of course." Her round face was grave, and she lowered her voice to a confidential murmur. "Such a comfort it was to have him with me when I was *enciente*, and during the confinement. When the pains were the worst, he held my hand and comforted me. I am sure he will do the same by you, when the time comes."

Horrour and disgust took Miranda's breath away. She prayed that she might faint, because her agony was too great to endure. Somehow she managed to rise, and without a word to her tormentor or anyone else, she escaped from the drawing-room. Dazed and sick, she paused in the hall, oblivious to the footmen as they removed the glasses and empty decanters from the dining-room.

Justin had fathered Princess Levaskov's baby son. The child's straight brown hair, those near-brown eyes—how blind she had been not to see the resemblance!

As if from a long way off, she heard Damon say, "I thought you were going to accompany me on the pianoforte. What did that devil's daughter say to make you bolt?" She did not answer his query, but let him guide her to an anteroom hung with enormous tapestries which depicted jousting knights and minstrels and ladies in pointed headdresses. "You will tell me what has happened, Mira, or I swear I'll choke it out of her," he said harshly.

"The little boy—Ivan," she whispered. "He's Justin's son. I ought to have guessed. I knew he was born months after her husband died."

"That's no proof that Justin sired him."

"She told me . . . or tried to. He was there for the birth. He held her hand. Oh, Damon, how can I bear this?"

He held her close against his chest while she wept, but he had no words of comfort; all he could do was let her sob her pain into his waistcoat. He damned his cousin, the most unfeeling brute alive, for hurting a girl so vulnerable to slights, and one whose emotions ran very near the surface.

At last the storm was spent. Miranda looked up, her elegant coiffure in disarray, looking so frightened that it wrung his heart. "You must be brave, *chérie*," he murmured, before pressing his cheek against her pale, damp one. Then he heard footsteps from behind, and fear snaked down his spine. Turning his head, he saw Justin standing in the doorway.

"I'll thank you to keep your hands off my bride."

Damon released Miranda at once, and in the moment she most needed the support of his arms, she was denied it. Justin's face was rigid with anger, almost unrecognisable. She couldn't find the words to explain that Damon had been trying to soothe the sorrows he had caused. Not knowing what else to do, she fled, brushing past him without acknowledging his presence.

Justin continued to glare at his cousin. "Are you so hot for her that you can't even wait until after the wedding to make me a cuckold?"

"Who are you to cast stones?" Damon challenged him. "Your hypocrisy sickens me, Justin, and your pretence of being the lovesick bridegroom is wearing thin. I knew you for what you are—a blackguard, and a mercenary one at that."

"You seem to be under the mistaken impression that I'm at fault," Justin said, his eye stony. "*I'm* not the one who has been caught in a compromising position with another man's fiancée. If you want her so much, why couldn't you marry her? She adores you and you love her, and I wish the pair of you had never brought me into it!"

"You can be sure I wouldn't have done, if I'd known of the nature of your attachment to the predatory princess," Damon retaliated. "You ought to warn her to be more discreet. Or don't you care that she goes spilling your foul secrets to those who will be most hurt by them?"

"As I haven't the least idea what you're talking about, I can't say."

"Oh, that's very good indeed," said Damon. "Your air of outraged innocence might convince Mira, but it leaves me unmoved."

"Do you think I'll seek consolation from Natasha when you and my wife consummate your *grande passion*? If you mean to give me horns as a wedding gift, you'll regret it, for I'll not be as complaisant as the pitiful husbands of all your other flames. Keep your distance from Miranda!"

Damon regarded him in silence for the space of several seconds. "Do you mean to say that Princess Levaskov is *not* your mistress?"

"And never has been."

"Oh lord," said Damon under his breath, "now here's a coil wants unravelling. But it was the little Russian herself who told Mira she had that brat of hers from *you*."

"And Miranda believed her?"

Damon nodded. "You had already prepared her to believe the worst by saying you had a confession to make. What did you mean by it?"

"Nothing so dire as the admission of a love-child," Justin said, and he couldn't help but smile. "I was going to tell her that I've decided against a career in the diplomatic service." Sobering, he continued, "What's to be done?"

"I'm sure I don't know," his cousin said unhelpfully. "Whenever I become involved in your affairs, I somehow manage to do more harm than good. Frankly, Justin, when she first refused you I thought she was well rid of you, and sometimes I am still of that opinion. You neglect her for weeks on end; you consort with another woman under her very nose and are as spiteful a member of the sex as I've encountered. If you have a care for Mira, you might at least tell her so."

"I don't see that it's any business of yours."

"Jealous? Well, it serves you right to be paid back in your own coin." Laughing softly, Damon walked out of the room.

Justin heard the sound of crumpling paper and looked down to see that his fist had closed around a letter. A footman had delivered it to him a few minutes earlier, and he had carried it out of the drawing-room to read it in private. Sitting down in the nearest chair, he felt his coat for his spectacles and settled them on his nose. His note came from Lord Granville, who wrote: "My dear Justin, I have married an angel. If you are even a tenth as happy with your Miranda as I expect to be with my Harriet, you will be fortunate indeed. My congratulations on the occasion of your marriage. G.L.C."

Justin let the letter fall and placed his head between his hands, wishing tomorrow were already behind him.

=13=

MIRANDA WAS ALREADY awake when Agnes Bleaklow parted the bed curtains, and at the sight of the abigail's tearful face she was seized by the paralysing certainty that Justin had cried off and there would be no wedding.

"Time to rise, my lady," Agnes told her softly. "They're already breakfasting belowstairs. I've brought up a morsel with your tea. You mayn't want it, but you'll do better to eat."

Miranda's panic subsided, and she tried to please Agnes by swallowing two cups of tea and some bread and butter, but she tasted none of it. She kept her eyes fixed upon the clock; the ceremony would commence at nine, and this last hour of her maidenhood would be the longest of her life.

Had Justin ever cared for her, or had he chosen her because he wanted to earn his wealthy uncle's goodwill and be rid of his mortgages? Back in the halcyon days before the princess and his child had come to England, his determined wooing had so nearly convinced her that their marriage would be founded on affection. But she couldn't dwell on that now, or she'd run the risk of disgracing herself at her own wedding. A fit of hysterics would convince Justin—and the world—that she was indeed her mother's daughter.

She climbed out of bed and untied her frilled nightcap so her maid could begin the ritual of combing the tangles from her hair. Opening one of the drawers in her mahogany dressing stand, she withdrew a silver locket. "I want you to accept this." Her spirits rose when she saw how pleased Agnes was by the gift. She turned out all of the drawers so that the contents might be packed.

"And what jewels will your ladyship wear today?" Agnes asked.

"The sapphire drops my uncle gave me for my coming of age." On the day Justin had walked into her life, she thought with a pang. "And this." She reached for her betrothal ring, and as she looked at the great blue stone set in a circle of brilliants, she was reminded how Justin had once said her eyes outshone it.

Her aunt and Nerissa soon came to see her dressed and readied. The white satin gown was lovely and made her look like a queen, but it felt cool and unfamiliar against her skin.

The duchess arranged the square of Mechlin lace on Miranda's head and fixed it with a diamond-studded hair-pin. "I wish your mother might see you," she said, patting one white cheek.

"So do I," Miranda whispered.

"Imogen and Ophelia arrived last night, after you retired," Nerissa told her. "Lord Hethington escorted them from town, as Imogen's husband was detained and couldn't come."

Miranda kept her eyes fixed on her reflexion in the looking glass. "I was feeling weary. Did it cause comment?"

"I don't think anyone noticed. Cousin William and Mr. Meriden settled down to a game of chess, and the princess and Lady Cavender talked about Justin. Nick and I sat in the corner with Cousin Elizabeth. He read the paper while we amused ourselves by tearing the princess's character to shreds."

"Nerissa, I did no such thing," the duchess said severely.

"You said she was tiresome, and that if she were so fond of Russia she'd have done better to stay there." Nerissa handed her cousin the sapphire ear-drops. "I'm not sure what became of Justin and Damon. They left the drawing-room as suddenly as you and weren't seen again till they appeared at the breakfast table. I imagine they were bored with the company and chose to play billiards."

When it was time to go downstairs Miranda took one long, last look at the creature in the mirror, who bore no resemblance to herself, then followed the others out of the room.

The household servants had collected along a corridor to watch the bride go by, and a long line of footmen in dress livery stood before the arched wooden doors of the chapel.

The duke was waiting, and when he had kissed Miranda, he smiled down at her and said, "The next time I do that, you'll be a viscountess."

The chapel was still decked out for Christmas and smelled of wax candles and evergreens. Justin had entered through another way with the chaplain and Lord Blythe, his groomsman. His best blue coat was complemented by a fine new waistcoat with gold embroidery, and he wore white breeches. He had sufficient time to assess the company assembled beneath the high, vaulted ceiling, and he nodded at his mother and uncle, together in a front pew. Across the aisle sat the duke's daughters, one tall and the other not, with a gentleman between them. Young Ninian was beside them, looking very solemn. Then his eye flickered past Natasha to rest upon the inscrutable white mask which was Damon's face.

The doors to the chapel opened, and the Duke of Solway entered, Miranda on his arm. Justin saw only the figure in bridal white as it came towards him, the black head covered with lace and slightly bowed. Even in the dim candlelight he could see that her cheeks were colourless, but her eyes were dry, and then he remembered that she had wept all her tears onto her true love's breast last night. Now she was perfectly composed, with no trace of emotion about her.

They met at the altar and faced the chaplain.

"Dearly beloved," Mr. Penfield intoned, his mellifluous voice doing justice to the occasion, "we are gathered together here in the sight of God and in the face of this congregation, to join together this man and woman in Holy Matrimony. . . ."

When Justin was asked if he would love, comfort, honour, and keep Miranda, and forsake all others, he swore that he would. He held his breath waiting for her response, but she did not fail him. The duke stepped back, and when Mr. Penfield had placed the bride's cool hand in the groom's hot one, the service proceeded.

After the exchange of vows, the couple knelt at the rail to receive the blessing. Mr. Penfield read a psalm, then led the congregation in the Lord's Prayer, and after an exhaustive selection of other prayers, Justin led his wife into an adjoining room to sign the register. The chapel bell began to peal loudly, startling Miranda, and her hand jerked so sharply that the pen showered ink across the page.

The number of guests had swelled by the time the wedding party arrived in the hall, where the wedding breakfast had been laid out. Neighbours and tenants had come, and there was a flurry of kissing and congratulations. When Damon detached Miranda from her husband's side and whispered something which made her smile, Justin concentrated on the distant chiming of church bells in the valley. There was a bride cake, and fowls and hams and custards in abundance. He had no appetite, having eaten only two hours earlier, but he accepted a glass of champagne. Wines and cordials made the rounds; footmen were kept busy filling glasses as toast after merry toast was drunk.

He was feeling more harassed than joyful when his uncle drew him apart from the throng and asked to speak to him in private. They went together into a small chamber hung with tapestries, the same one in which Justin had surprised Damon and Miranda.

"I'm glad for you, my boy," said Mr. Meriden. "Such a wife as yours will, I warrant you, bear a strong, fine brood and ensure the continuance of an ancient title."

The succession was not foremost in Justin's thoughts

at that particular moment, but he nodded and mumbled something appropriate.

"You will recall the pact we made, just after your return from abroad," his uncle continued, going to the mantel shelf to take up a stack of papers lying there. Brandishing them, he said, "Your mortgages, Justin. I gave you my word, and I'm honour-bound to do as I said I would, for you've fulfilled the condition of our bargain."

The parchments represented nearly one hundred thousand pounds of indebtedness, and the sight of them afforded Justin little pleasure. He watched in silence as his benefactor fed the top sheet to the flames. The rest followed, one by one.

A movement near the door made him look around, and he saw Miranda standing on the threshold, also observing the destruction of the deeds. At least, he thought, she did not know the significance of what to her must seem a curious ceremony.

In this he was wrong. Miranda knew only too well: he had won his freedom from debt by entering into another, more durable form of bondage. And he looked so unhappy, she thought, as if he had regrets already.

"Lady Cavender!" Nerissa cried out. Vaguely aware that it was she who had been hailed, Miranda went to her. "Oughtn't you to go to change? Justin told Nick he wanted to be away by half past ten, and it's nearly that now."

"Yes, of course," she murmured, and tried to banish the hurtful memory of her husband's trapped expression.

The destruction of the parchments took a considerable time and made an unpleasant smell. Justin could not walk away from this ritual which obviously meant so much to his uncle, though he longed for it to end.

"There," Mr. Meriden said, placing the last sheet in the fire, "that's done it." He dusted his hands with his handkerchief, saying heartily, "Have a safe, swift journey to the Chase, my boy, and bring your lady to Bath when you grow weary of the country."

He left Justin to watch the final sheet crumple and blacken in the grate, until it was reduced to ashes, like the hopes he had brought with him to Haberdine. Now that Miranda was his, he had already lost her to Damon, so polished, so dashing, through a fatal combination of selfish neglect and Natasha's destructive falsehoods. Those whom he had believed to be his friends had turned out to be his bitterest enemies, and during a sleepless night he had resolved to carve them out of his life.

His mournful reverie was broken by the entrance of the last person he wanted to see. Damon joined him, a glass of champagne in his hand, and his drawling voice was tinged with sarcasm when he said, "I can't think why the luckiest man on this earth should be standing all alone, scowling into the fire."

Justin wasn't about to confide his woes to the one who had caused so many of them. "It's none of your concern," he said stiffly.

"No?" Damon shrugged. "I found your princess crying in a dark corridor just now, and I don't think it was from joy. My experience in soothing your lovelorn victims stood me in good stead, and when she was restored to calm I offered to escort her back to town. She's not likely to fling herself at me in her present state of despondency, which is just as well. I'm in no mood for dalliance."

Of course not, Justin thought furiously, he was content to bide his time until he could lure Miranda from her husband's bed to his. "I don't care what you do, or Natasha either. In future she must depend upon the Pembrokes for company. I don't know when I shall return to London."

As Damon digested this, a smile lurked at the corners of his mouth. "Poor little Mira, I would pity her if I didn't suspect that being stuck at Cavender Chase with her sadly misguided husband is probably just her taste. Treat her kindly, Justin, and perhaps I'll forgive you for all those horrid accusations you flung at me last night."

When Miranda came downstairs in a rose velvet pelisse trimmed with fur and a matching hat, all of her relatives clamoured for farewell kisses.

Ninian forced his way to her side and gripped her hand. "I want to visit your new house."

She knelt down and pinched his cheek. "Of course you will, during your Easter holiday. And I promise I'll have a lovely surprise for you."

"If you haven't decided yet what it's to be, I desperately need a boat of my own," he told her.

Placing her lips near his ear, she whispered, "It won't be a boat, but a person. Ask Uncle William to tell you who, when he comes to your room to bid you goodnight."

She walked out into the grey dampness on her husband's arm. The chaise, a new one, waited at the bottom of the steps; it had the Cavender crest on the panel, surmounted by a viscount's coronet. The jewellery case, the foxhounds, and the baggage had been placed in a hired vehicle which would also carry Agnes Bleaklow.

Miranda embraced her aunt one last time and received a damp kiss from her mother-in-law. Then she and Justin climbed into the chaise, and the postboys spurred their mounts. They moved slowly along the drive at first, but after passing through the bastion towers, the carriage picked up speed. As it followed the turnpike road to Lutterworth, Miranda and Justin talked of the wedding, in an artificial manner that overlay the constraint between them. After the excellence of the breakfast had been discussed, and the lavishness of the bride-gifts was exhausted as a topic, they ran out of things to say.

Interrupting a long and oppressive period of silence, Justin said, "If you wish to sleep, don't think you must refrain on my account."

Miranda assumed that he was weary of her nervous chattering, and leaned her head against the seat-back. The motion of the chaise was hardly soothing or conducive to sleep. She would be far more comfortable resting against his shoulder, but could not assert herself to that extent. In his present mood, which was quite unlike any she had experienced, he might well shove her aside.

At times during the day she gave up her pretence of dozing to gaze through her window and the villages along the way. Each time they stopped for a change of horses, or to walk the dogs, Justin ordered whatever refreshment she desired. Once, while waiting for a fresh team to be harnessed, he suggested that they stretch their legs. They strolled the high street of a quiet hamlet, which ended at the lych-gate of a small church. Tacked to the side of the wooden awning was a paper with the names of the local couples whose banns had been cried at the service that morning. After reading it, Justin and Miranda returned to the chaise to continue the long and punishing drive.

=14=

IT WAS LATE when the newlyweds reached their destination. Miranda, hearing the deep, persistent toll of a church bell, asked, "Have your people stayed up to welcome us? It must be near midnight."

"Exactly that," Justin said, after consulting his watch.

As the death knell of 1809 sounded, Miranda's eyes sought the shadowed face of the man who had become her husband that morning. He was as much as stranger now as he'd been at her birthday ball so many moths ago.

The chaise halted and its lamps threw a faint light upon the façade of the house. Justin climbed out first, then helped Miranda down before giving orders about their baggage. The sleepy hounds tumbled out of the second carriage, sniffing the unfamiliar ground. "Take them to the stables," Justin told a groom before ushering Miranda up the steps and into their home. Agnes, carrying the jewellery case, followed at a respectful distance.

A few servants gathered in the hall to greet their master and mistress. One man, whose lack of livery indicated that he was the new steward, announced that a supper was ready to be served if they wanted it. When Miranda nodded, Justin suggested that they repair to the dining-room at once. Several leaves had been removed from long table since their earlier visit, and when Miranda sat down in the place formerly occupied by her predecessor, she was at no great distance from Justin. They were waited on by the steward, who vanished after serving them and reappeared only to carry away the plates. Too weary to be much interested in food, Miranda had only nibbled at a piece of roast chicken, but she nodded when the man offered to refill her glass with wine.

Justin had set her lack of appetite down to apprehension, and as soon as they were alone again, he said, "You have no cause to be afraid." Only twenty-four hours ago she'd sought Damon's embrace, and she must shrink at the prospect of giving herself to another man. "I think we ought to decide now how we mean to go on," he told her. "If I demand that you break with Damon, can you do so?"

"Break with him?" she asked, frowning. "Why, have you quarrelled?"

"Last night," he said pointedly, and was sorry for it when she winced as though he'd struck her.

Her voice was heavy with fatigue as she said, "I was distraught. The princess had just named you as father of her son. Damon offered me comfort, only that, and I had need of it. My lord, you've played me false."

"Dear love, I would not for the world."

"I cannot be soothed with lies, Justin." Her eyes flashed with blue fire, and with the recollection of her grievances her flagging energy revived. "Nor can I make it easier for you by pretending I'm not hurt by your . . . your liaison, or the fact that you flaunted it before me and all my family."

"I did no such thing! Natasha was never my mistress, not while I lived in Russia, and certainly not since she has been in England. All those weeks I was too busy worrying about the Persian treaty, trying to prove myself to the Foreign Office, to realise what mischief Natasha was about. I was blind to her strategems and deaf to her cruel innuendo."

"But the child—you were with her when he was born."

"She said that? Miranda, on my honour I swear to you that I wasn't even at Droskoe during her confinement. I'd gone out wolf-hunting with her brother, Prince Nikolai. And I didn't sire Ivanushka, who is Prince Paul

Levaskov's true son and was conceived before his father fell ill. Do you really think me the sort to cuckold my own best friend?"

"Well, you obviously thought me the sort to cuckold you with your own cousin," she retorted. "As if I could, when I'm in—" She broke off, and after a glance at his expectant face she substituted another reason. "I'm very fond of Damon and always shall be. He has been my firm friend through many trials. But he would be as uncomfortable a lover as he would be a husband. He cares only for himself, apart from being wholly incapable of fidelity and a true and lasting affection."

"And were you hoping I could offer those things, Miranda?"

To beg for his love was as impossible as admitting hers; she had too much pride. "I had a fancy to be wed," she told him quietly. "I was lonely and wanted companionship, I was tired of living in a house which was not my own. You chose me because you hoped to please your uncle and wished to be rid of your mortgages." She saw that he was taken aback, and her mention of his debt had brought a flush to his face. "We would appear to be well-matched, don't you agree?" she asked, rising from her chair. "Now I must beg you to excuse me, as it has been a tiring sort of day." Her limbs were stiff from the long hours in the chaise, and her exit was not as smooth or as speedy as she would have preferred.

When she reached her candlelit chamber, she found Agnes waiting to help her undress as if nothing out of the ordinary had occurred since she'd performed the same office the night before. Miranda put on her new nightgown, a fine, soft cotton with a low neck and long sleeves ending in a ruffle. It made her feel exposed and uncomfortable, and she quickly covered herself with a wrapper.

Agnes unbound her hair and combed it out, occasionally pausing to pat Miranda's shoulder, as if to offer reassurance. "Would your ladyship be wanting a glass of warm milk?"

175

This offer, which Miranda hadn't heard since her nursery days, elicited a smile. "I think not. Thank you, Agnes, that will be all."

"Good-night, my lady."

When the abigail left her, Miranda found herself drawn to the large bed where the next confrontation in this curious day-old marriage of hers would occur, and her fingers traced the colourful flowers and butterflies her mother had embroidered upon the yellow counterpane. Here she would receive her husband; this was where their children would be born. But she was not daring enough to wait for her tardy bridegroom between the covers, so she sought the comfort of a couch facing the fireplace.

The princess had never been Justin's mistress; he had no son. He'd said so, and she believed him. If only she had asked him sooner, she thought, how much heartache she would have been spared! He must care—he had helped her to face the fears she had kept hidden even from her aunt and uncle, and he had reunited her with her mother. He had tutored her in passion and cured her forever of the desire to make a marriage founded on convenience.

The Jubilee year had closed with the tolling of bells, those marking her marriage and those which had designated the end of 1809. She was beginning the new year with a different name in a new home, without any secrets standing between her and Justin and ought to be glad of that, but her mind was numb with exhaustion.

The house was silent and still around her; the wine she'd drunk and the warmth of the fire conspired to make her drowsy. She reclined upon the sofa and used its armrest as a pillow, never intending to sleep, but soon she fell into a welcome state of unconsciousness.

She was wakened by the crackle and hiss of the fire, and her eyes flew open. Justin knelt on the hearth-rug, wielding the poker. Gone were his blue coat and gold-threaded waistcoat, and he'd removed his cravat; the white shirt gaped open at the neck and his wristbands were undone. "You looked so peaceful I hated to disturb you," he said, looking over at her. "But you will not want to spend what's left of the night there."

"I suppose not," she murmured, closing her eyes again.

"The mortgages," he went on in a low voice, as if no time had passed since she'd left the dining-room so abruptly, "I wonder how you knew about them, for I never told you. Was it Damon? Did he tell you last night?"

"No, whole months ago. Just before you proposed to me—the first time."

"And today, when you saw Uncle Isaac put those papers on the fire, it confirmed your belief that I married you at his command."

"It doesn't matter any longer, Justin."

"To me it does. You must have despised me."

She sat up. "I never did!"

"Mercenary, cold-blooded, selfish, unfaithful—how could you marry such a one?"

"Because I love you." His self-congratulatory smile told her he'd intended her to make that confession. "That was a low trick," she said, but without heat. "A lawyer's trick."

"It was," he agreed, sitting down beside her and taking her hand. "When I arrived at Haberdine I had something to tell you and never got the chance. I've parted company with the Foreign Office. My work, not Natasha, was my mistress. I'm sorry to shatter your dreams of a brilliant Tory salon, but henceforth my involvement with politics will be confined to an occasional appearance in the House of Lords. And even that is likely to take second place to putting Cavender Chase in order."

"Country living will work no hardship upon me, Justin." She returned the warm pressure of his fingers. "London houses are expensive, and my dowry could be put to better use until the estate shows a profit."

"That will not be so very long, now I'm free of the mortgages." When her face clouded over, he traced her cheekbone and said gently, "I didn't have to marry you. There are ladies blessed with fortunes large enough to swallow my debt many times over. I might have told my uncle to go to the devil and found myself an heiress with more than fifty thousand pounds. But I didn't. I couldn't. From the moment we met I wanted you and no other. It's true that Uncle Isaac bought up the mortgages and held them over my head to make me offer for you. To him, money is a means of purchasing affection and gratitude. And he has bought mine, never doubt that, although it has nothing to do with what you observed this morning. If you truly believe I married you for any other reason than from a hopeless inability to live without you, you're greatly mistaken. You are my whole life now, Miranda, and mean far more to me than bricks and mortar or a career as a diplomat."

"I wish you had told me," she sighed. "You never spoke of love and honour and forsaking all others until we stood together in the chapel this morning."

"Only because I assumed my actions had been sufficient to convince you how I feel. Miranda, I've wooed you and wed you and sworn to be faithful. I've endowed you with all my worldly goods, however worthless they may seem. What more can I do to prove that you have all my heart?"

"This," she said, placing her eager mouth upon his, and for some time afterwards she devoted her attention to the pleasant task of convincing him of her good faith.

If you would like to receive details on other Walker Regency Romances, please write to:

Regency Editor
Walker and Company
720 Fifth Avenue
New York, NY 10019